The Architect

Brendan Connell

The Architect
by Brendan Connell

ISBN: 978-1-908125-08-8

Publication Date: January 2020

Originally published by PS Publishing in 2012
as a 300 copy limited edition

EibonVale
www.eibonvalepress.co.uk

The Architect

I.

"The Meeting Place . . ."

". . . needs to be something really special."

"These designs are all very competent, but . . ."

"???"

". . . they lack vision."

"But it seems to me that practicality . . ."

". . . the servant of human life."

"Practicality dirties the principle essence."

"That is going a bit far!"

"There is the matter of spiritual depth."

"Utility."

"But certainly we can find a compromise."

"Certainly—when we have something to compromise about!"

Like pebbles cast into a gloomy mountain pond, ideas were tossed about and words rippled across the room.

A pale and somewhat transcendental light came through white curtains which concealed four large windows. A huge framed portrait of Dr. Peter Körn (1849-1924), visionary, spiritual scientist, hung on one wall. Its sombre colouring, the stony gaze and chiselled features, carried with them the cold of caves, the brutishness of a troglodyte mixed with the ferocious cunning of a wolf. He had made a science of the human soul, indefatigably lectured his way across Europe, his prophetic and vivid experience, come upon under the influence of some faux-divine psychological, physiological state, lay somewhere between the dream and the nightmare, between bizarre and beautiful vistas, trillions of jewel-like worlds, and hoards of demons searing each other's mutilated flesh with red-hot instruments drawn from the fire of infernal pits.

A million busy spiders had been born from the cobwebs of his philosophies. His systems were oiled with the residue of ten-thousand fortunes, the trimmings of seemingly countless stipends. Theism has created many such hybrids, Frankensteins: the limbs of materialism stitched onto the anthropomorphic body of regeneration.

Four people (three men and one woman) stood around a large, glossy oak table. The men were grave-looking fellows, of varying size and height. The woman was light as a cloud.

These were the board members of the Society.

Large sheets of paper, with architectural designs, covered the table. The party cast their eyes over these collections of lines—a confusing array of cubes and eggs, arrows and measurements.

"What about this one, submitted by Mr. Mario Botta?"

Dr. Enheim smoothed his moustaches gravely.

"It simply doesn't strike me as holistic enough."

"And this proposition by Mr. Yokotoko of Japan?"

"Far too modern," said the woman. "It leaves me cold."

Sheathed in an emerald-coloured silk dress, she was somewhat over forty years of age, though she could have passed for thirty. Though not pretty, she was beautiful, just as certain liquors are not pleasant to drink but none the less produce strong intoxication. Her name was Maria Venezuela. She was of strong intelligence and a highly mystical bent of mind. An advocate of homeopathic medicine and flower essences, a dabbler in massage, her public profession was that of aroma therapist—though in fact she was, through her family, independently wealthy and had no need to struggle to survive; could choose her clients, dispensing phytoncides and sassafras, marjoram and melaleuca where and when she wished.

She was a type not uncommon in today's world. A sort of white witch, well versed in chakra theory, the secret life of Jesus and the works of Franz Mesmer.

But her passion was Körn.

"Let us face it," she said, "they are all horrible. One looks like an office building, the next a bank."

"From a woman's point of view, it is possible that——"

"From a woman's point of view?" she snarled, her white teeth flashing dangerously between the bright red petals of her lips. "Can you seriously tell me then that the rest of you approve of these monstrosities? Are you really going to let the followers of Dr. Körn meet, to learn about sacred and profound things, in some common-place structure that takes after a house of commerce? These designs reek of materialism while what we need is something that will uplift our souls!"

"Bravo, dear lady!" Dr. Enheim cried in his baritone voice. "What you have said is very true. Dr. Körn himself would never have approved of these designs. In his 1914 lecture on architecture at the University of Göttingen he said that great architecture transforms the world of material objects into a direct and immutable projection of the spirit. The current projects before us, on the other hand, seem . . . all too mundane."

The men stood stranded in a minute of silence. A minute of silence which we will artfully take advantage of by briefly describing them.

Dr. Herman Enheim was tall, extremely stout, possessed of a belly as formidable as his intelligence. His large beard, which was raven-black despite his fifty some odd years, lent him the air of a figure out of the Old Testament—a sort of over-larded Moses—a man who, from the depths of that forest of hair, spoke to the people with the voice of a prophet. Never smiling, with a steady, eagle-like gaze shielded by two lush black eyebrows, he commanded immediate respect upon entering a room.

His list of academic credentials was long. He spoke half a dozen European languages perfectly. It was said that he also knew Japanese and Sanskrit. In his conversation, he sometimes quoted from the Mahabharata. He had meditated on the banks of the Ganges and prayed at Mary's tomb in Jerusalem.

He was the world's foremost authority on Körn philosophy, and therefore, quite rightfully, the president of the Society, Commander Adeptus Magus. He gave long, ponderous lectures several times a week. The audience, particularly the women, would gaze at him in rapture, their ears quivering as they were brushed by the deep, romantic intonations of his voice. A remarkable number of the females of his flock were in love with him. But his weakness, if it could be called such, was not for the opposite sex, but for the adventures of the kitchen. He was an impressive cook, a redoubtable eater—a man who had been initiated into the mysteries of the soufflé and had sacrificed many a leporidae at the altar of his stomach.

Next comes Valentino Borromeo. A man with a face that seemed as if it had been carved out of wood. His athletic figure made him look good in any suit of clothes. In his youth he had won the Giro di Lombardia and though now a man in his mid-forties, he was still remarkably fit. A head of short, black hair, the temples of which were slightly dusted with grey, relaxed behind a reclining hairline. A sharply-cut nose lent his face a certain noble quality and he could have legitimately been called handsome.

He had come to Körn at the age of thirty-six, after being confronted by the impermanence of an athletic career, and was now as adamant a follower as any, studying the philosophy with the same regularity and perseverance he had previously used in training for the great bicycle races of Europe—pumping up his spiritual muscles with the weighty doctrines of the German sage, spinning the humble gears of his mind along the curves of the track in the hopes of reaching some indistinguishable finishing line.

Finally, there was Daniel Nesler, a short, thin, balding individual with eyeglasses and yellow skin—one of those entities whose clothes never seem to fit them. His pants and jackets were always too large and the collars of his shirts too small, while, due to the short nature of his arms, the sleeves covered up half his hands which groped about like sea-anemones. Though he was quite well off, he would not buy his clothes from a tailor, but insisted on buying them off the ready-made sales racks—where the sizes were inevitably all wrong for his mutant physique. Though naturally unintelligent, he was possessed with a formidable energy, so that he often surpassed much greater men. When given a task, he worked tirelessly at it, with the energy of a rodent and the industriousness of an ant.

"But then what are we to do?" he now pouted. "We have been going over proposals for months, and eventually we need to make a decision. Either that, or renounce the project altogether."

Maria glanced at the slim-banded gold watch that adorned her wrist.

"Patience," she said.

"Patience?"

"Knowledge comes with waiting," she pronounced sententiously.

"But what are we waiting for?" Borromeo asked.

"He is coming just now."

The vague sound of outward footsteps could be heard. There was then a knock at the door.

"That will be my nephew."

"Your nephew?"

"Yes, he is, as you know, aside from being a dedicated follower of Körn philosophy, a student of architecture. He has certain ideas of his own which I have asked him to come here and present."

The men gazed at each other uneasily while Maria opened the door.

A young man entered. His longish, oily black hair was parted in the middle, forming two wings which flanked a large, pale forehead. A pair of gold, wire-rimmed glasses sat on a rather long nose, and his lips, thin and dry as two wisps of straw, were stretched above a frail and clean-shaven chin which was slightly cleft.

Peter de la Tour was one of those solemn young men who, unable to find gratification in the frolics of those their own age, open wide their arms and embrace the cold pillars of knowledge. A student of architecture, he studied the subject with the same sort of vehemence as a religious fanatic would the words of scripture. He looked for salvation in the designs of Eero Saarinen and Walter Gropius and worshipped not God, but rather the Sullivanesque style of the Wainright building, Gothic arches and flying buttresses, and those steeples of glass found in New York and Paris which mirror both sky and earth. He had let his mind absorb three-thousand years of theory as a dry desert would a sudden burst of rain. He was interested in the esoteric mystery of the art.

Some look for salvation in religion. Some cast themselves wholeheartedly into hell by means of great crimes. A few seclude themselves from the world by living in caves or huts in the forest. Others let their bodies be swept along by the crowd and are glad to live like other men—many rich finding their way by means of gluttonous excess; many poor making cockroaches their art, their science. But then there is another breed, the eccentrics, who, discontent with the crowded thoroughfares, yet not attracted by the paths which lead through the deep canyons of asceticism, take a different way. Mozart climbed to the heights of the universe along slim ladders of musical notes. Michelangelo chiselled through countless blocks of marble to reach divinity. And there are the million others who no one has heard of. Men who dedicate themselves to the study of prairie grasses. Women whose smiles commit suicide as the tall clock in the gallery strikes midnight. People who defy easy categorisation as there has not yet been a symbolic system invented that can define centipedes in human form, roses who speak in cafés, young men with minds of masonry and glass.

Peter's arms, which were those of a thinker rather than a labourer (that is to say thin), were dragged taut by a huge tome which he heaved onto the table.

"I have brought an interesting document to share with you gentleman."

He opened the book and the scent of mildew, long-dead cigars and verbena filled the room.

"I am not sure I understand . . ." Borromeo began.

Nesler shrugged his shoulders impatiently.

"Please, my friends," Maria said, "I beg you to be open-minded. This is a matter of evolution."

"The young man has my attention," Dr. Enheim conceded graciously.

"If you would care to look . . ." Peter murmured.

The men gathered round, dipped their noses between the great pages which displayed themselves open-armed, like crucified saints.

Thoughts can be as powerful as fists, a drawing more violent than a bomb, a single line as spacious as a city. Books, those warehouses of consciousness, are able to reach out across space and time and grab, caress, even force. There is nothing more dangerous, more sublime than a few hundred or a thousand pages fastened together and sandwiched between protective covers.

Peter remained silent. The pictures spoke—chanted, screamed, and fell into caressing whispers.

Huge edifices, megastructures, poured from the leaves. Bridges which spanned oceans, towers which stretched into the clouds, huge fortresses which looked as if they could withstand the destructive force of an Armageddon. Vertical cities rose up from desert plains in startling anaxometrics, while spatial cities, cities built fifteen or twenty meters above their counterparts, stood forth as visions of utopian architecture, only to be outdone on subsequent pages by floating cities, vast nests of hexagonal pods resting atop lakes and oceans. Structures which straddled the earth and others which burrowed under it. Buildings which brought to mind lost civilizations or seemed to be the habitations of beings from another world.

Maria Venezuela's eyes gleamed with an enigmatic light. Nesler licked his thin lips greedily. Borromeo stood solemn, his face noble—like that of Alexander gazing off towards the unknown lands of Asia that he felt impelled to conquer.

Dr. Enheim turned towards Peter. "What is this you have brought us?"

"It is a very rare book, privately printed twenty years ago in an edition of only fifty copies."

"And who is the architect?"

"His name is Alexius Nachtman."

"I have never heard of him."

"Very few have. It is only chance that brought this book into my hands at a flea market in Milan. You can imagine how it fired my enthusiasm!"

"I can."

"When I first saw it, I was left speechless."

"The designs are magnificent."

"True mystery and grandeur," Borromeo commented, flexing his arm.

"The language of this book, a language without words," said Maria in a soft and charming voice, "strikes me as the language of deep spirituality . . ."

It was only Nesler who objected, straightening his back, repulsing his initial attraction to the fascinating designs with a scepticism that seemed pronged with arithmetic, prickly with narrow logic.

"This is all very fine, as far as science fiction goes," he said, "but I do not really see what it has to do with the subject at hand, that is the Meeting Place."

"I was under the impression that you were accepting proposals for the design," Peter calmly stated.

"And we are. We are accepting serious proposals from serious architects."

"And how would you define serious?"

"That which does not incite laughter. Free from extravagance."

"Great men, great artists, are never free from extravagance. And, though it might be bold of me to say, Dr. Körn himself was not without this quality and was in fact accused by his detractors of many follies."

"What the young man says is true," Borromeo put in. "Maybe it is because I am Italian, but I must say that I would prefer to have with us someone with a certain artistic flair. A sense of adventure is not a bad thing."

Peter pushed his glasses to the back of his nose. "When I suggested to my aunt that you might consider Herr Nachtman, she was not opposed to the idea."

"I was not," she said. "And, seeing that there seems to be some measure of interest, I propose that we ask Mr. Nachtman to submit a design for the Meeting Place."

"But this is the work of a madman!" Nesler cried out, waving his thin arm at the great book.

"No, it is the work of a visionary!" Peter responded.

"The only difference between a madman and a visionary is that the latter creates what the former only dreams of. After all, what has this man actually built? Theoretical architecture is one thing, reality another."

"It would be interesting to see the physical work he has done," Enheim added.

"My understanding," Peter replied, "is that his actual portfolio of finished buildings is, um, somewhat limited due to his, um, political beliefs."

"Ah, then we cannot waste any more time on this nonsense," Nesler cried in a sharp voice.

"Mr. Nesler," Dr. Enheim said, "I understand that you consider yourself to be the voice of reason in this assembly. But I fear you are forgetting one of the principal tenets of the Society. We are open to all. Surely if this Nachtman were to be interested in, were to be willing to submit a proposal, we should condescend to consider it. We must follow our own divine impulses and not let our egos impede us on the path to knowledge."

II.

Dr. Maxwell Körn had been born the son of the German composer Arthur Carl Körn, better known as Hans Johann, a figure virtually unknown today but who, in the 1840s, had a brief celebrity for his work *Salmoneus*, a series of linked sonatas for arpeggione and piano. Little is known of his mother, though Körn himself stated her to be an extremely pious woman who, while in church, was often taken with fits of trembling. She died while he was still young, of an overdose of strychnine which had been prescribed by a homeopathic physician.

Possessed of piercing black eyes and a mane of chestnut-coloured hair, young Körn had an intensity about him that few failed to notice. When he entered a room all eyes turned to him. Even those who disliked him admired him, and those who liked him loved him.

He studied under Professor Brockhaus at the University of Leipzig, and also under Schelling; was highly interested in comparative mythology and is said during this period to have been heavily influenced by the *Philokalia*, particularly those portions written by Saint Gregory Palamas. Undoubtedly these early Christian writers provided him with inspiration and set a foundation upon which the mighty fort of his philosophy would later be built.

Through unhappy speculation pertaining to the Ottoman Empire, his father went bankrupt and was unable to support his son. The latter took up the life of a poor student, maintaining himself by translating, giving lessons in Hebrew and Greek, and writing newspaper articles.

At the age of twenty-one, out of necessity, he published a short novel titled *Die Toten Augen von Mars*, which dealt with themes of spiritualism and romance, describing a visionary journey made by a young couple around the solar system and talked of the spiritual inhabitants of other planets. It was an immediate success, particularly amongst society women, launching young Körn, giving him entrance into fashionable Thursday evenings and opening the doors of the better clubs for gentlemen.

For the next few years he lived the life of a bon vivant, became passionately fond of gambling and developed a taste for fine horseflesh. He wore a coat with a thick fur collar and bought himself a number of rare paintings by Altdorfer. He visited houses of prostitution, fought duels, kept mistresses, and spent greatly beyond his means, so that he was soon deeply in debt, was forced to hide himself. It is said that at times he went about disguised as a woman, at times resorted to wearing a false beard.

No longer was he seen at the fashionable soirees or in his box at the opera. For most it seemed as if he had disappeared completely, gone up in a puff of smoke or been taken up on a gust of wind like a djinn. Unceremoniously, without pomp and to the muffled drumbeat of rumour, a veiled period of his life was inaugurated. Some say he worked for the Prussian secret service, others that he smuggled diamonds, while a few averred that he had become involved in the slave trade.

According to his own accounts, he was studying under a master in Amsterdam, whom he was, for spiritual reasons, unable to name but who was a direct descendant of Paracelsus. After receiving certain occult initiations pertaining to the Order of the Hermetic Brotherhood from this gentleman, he left Europe, travelled in India, China and Tibet. He lunched with swamis and drank tea with Taoist sages, studying under no less than one-hundred different masters. He became adept at the art of snake charming, an expert in Unani medicine and entered a secret society of adepts where he studied the anatomy of the soul.

Upon returning to the west, he set himself vigorously to the task of writing articles and books, systemising the entire universe, both physical and spiritual, drawing from every science, culture and religion, contributing to numerous periodicals, including *Neue Welt*, *Die Gnosis* and *Die Sphinx*. He did phrenologic investigations of select individuals and espoused theories of cerebral inheritance. Attracting the attention of many wealthy patrons, most notably Franz Salvator, Archduke of Austria-Tuscany, he was soon provided with an annual stipend which allowed him to continue his studies with more leisure.

The consummation of his spirituality seems to have occurred on April 3rd, 1894, when, at the age of forty-two, he was sitting on the last wooden bench on platform number 3 of the Lehrter Bahnhof in Berlin. He had eaten a plate of roast beef an hour earlier. It was around 6:30 pm. Over the next twenty minutes he became spontaneously enlightened and understood the workings of the entire universe, from its creation to its future destruction and saw both the purpose of mankind and the purpose of life, the celestial scheme of things.

On March 5th, 1896, he declared that he would form a Universal Brotherhood of Mankind and, indeed, spent the rest of his days attempting to establish the new supramental consciousness on earth.

Unequivocally inspired, he lectured all over Europe, but found particularly strong welcome in the intellectual circles of Switzerland, Austria and Italy, where he addressed some of the largest audiences ever gathered to hear one man's thoughts on the religious meaning of life. In the year 1903 alone he was said to have given 291 lectures. He spoke on a vast variety of subjects, ranging from music to gardening, from Greek mythology to alphabetic dance. Occasionally during his discourses, he was known to slip into glossolalia, which he would afterwards apologize for.

- He entered into ecstatic trances in which his astral body visited other planets and planes, met with other beings, familiars and archangels, the souls of great thinkers. He reported on the states of hell and transcribed the teachings of various celestial attendants.
- He lived with a circle of close disciples from whom he demanded absolute obedience.
- He was said to have read the Bible, from beginning to end, once a year throughout his life.
- Certain journalistic organs accused him of charlatanism, pointing to the fact that he was in the habit of profusely adorning his fingers with costly rings and was known to supply his table with the most expensive wines and delicacies. These accusations he categorically refuted in his pamphlet Why Gold is God Too.

- In 1899, England's Society for Psychical Research (SPR), dispatched Dr. Richard Gibson to investigate the Society. Not only did this latter pronounce Körn to be absolutely innocent of fraud, but later went on to become one of his foremost disciples and was largely responsible for the introduction of Körn's work to the English speaking world, establishing centres in both London and Edinburgh.
- The last years of his life he spent largely in seclusion, translating the Akashic Records and often spending weeks at a time in self-imposed silence. Though this work was left unfinished, it was published in sixty-three volumes (Buchverlag der Taweret, Frankfurt 1924).

III.

It was a mellow and humid day in spring, atmosphere thick, sky smeared with a white froth of clouds. Peter, after making many inquiries, had managed to find the address of Nachtman. A small, mountain village with cobbled streets which was bordered by cows on green slopes, sheep masticating dandelions. One of those places where everyone knows the most minute habits of everyone else, the tranquillity of the day only broken by the occasional creaking of shutters or the lonely steps of an old man making his way to the cemetery to deposit a handful of wilted flowers where his heart lay buried.

A somewhat seedy stone structure with moss growing on the slate roof—vaguely Italianate—a faded fresco of a saint adorned the outer wall. Rusty gutters crawled from roof to pavement. A lazy balcony stretched out its tongue.

Peter knocked on a small door which was painted turquoise, but no one answered. A fat old woman appeared at the window of the adjacent house.

"Excuse me," the young man asked, "but is this the residence of Herr Nachtman?"

"A man lives there."

"Is he an architect?"

"I don't think so. A lecher maybe. A drunk most certainly. But an architect . . . no!"

"Are you positive?"

"I do not speak to him. I am an honest woman."

"He is not at home."

"Then he is undoubtedly at the bar," she said, thrusting her chin in a southerly direction.

Peter, after following this signalling device a short distance, found the place, entered, was accosted by the smell of ancient yeast and frying sausages.

A few voluble young men. A lumpy middle-aged woman with bright red hair. A television mounted above the bar. Football: dots running around a green field. At a small table in the corner two thin legs jutted out from beneath the barrier of an open newspaper. On the table was an almost empty glass of beer.

A frowsy looking waitress approached Peter.

"Sit wherever you want."

"I am looking for someone."

"And have you found her?"

"I am looking for a man. Nachtman."

"Nachtman?"

"Alexius Nachtman."

"Ah, you must mean Alex," she said, pointing to the corner, to the man who was foraging through the newspaper, now draining off the last of his beer.

Peter approached.

"Excuse me, but is your name Alexius Nachtman?"

The man looked up, shot a penetrating glance at the student.

"And if it was?"

"Then I would be delighted to make your acquaintance."

"I do not doubt it. But would I be delighted to make yours?"

Peter took note of the empty glass.

"May I buy you a beer?"

"You may," the other said, folding the paper in two and tossing it aside.

He was over fifty years old, had a large, compact torso, like the body of an owl, planted atop two spindly legs, like those of a stork. His arms were long and thick like an ape's. His nose was bulbous, red, as wrinkled as a prune. And from a muddy complexion, two small, dark eyes emitted a gaze as sharp as a needle. A skirt of wispy white hair fringed his skull, which was as knobby as the trunk of a hundred-year-old chestnut tree. He sneered more often than smiled, and his smile was more grotesque than his frown. It was a pit of irregular yellow rectangles, offset by two dull silver flashes, for his maxillary canine teeth were capped with a ductile metallic element. He had the appearance of a deformed root dug from the ground. He was remarkably ugly. But the greatest geniuses are rarely beautiful to look upon.

After ordering two beers, Peter commenced:

"I have been looking for you for some time."

"I see."

"I have been commissioned by the Körn Society to find you. I am in possession of your book, *Omegastructures.* Fascinating stuff. The Society is currently in need of a meeting place. They wish for a fitting structure to be built. They are currently considering proposals from a large range of architects and——"

"Architects? They have not existed for hundreds of years! The morons you see today building their feeble prostitutions are nothing more than rats in human form, gnawing at scraps of Vitruvius and gurgling the academic banalities of Alvar Aalto. Architecture is a lost science, buried with the Atlanteans. It is a word bandied about latrine-like universities—those places where, when originality occasionally shows its face, like the bloom of the century plant, it is instantly put to death, stoned like a blaspheming Naboth."

He leaned back in his chair, his ample belly pushed forward, and reached for the cylinder of beer before him. He drained half the glass at a draught and, after licking his pale and flaccid lips, continued:

"For long now has the human race been covering the earth with brutish structures, committing edificial sins and wallowing in an orgy of architectural shame. The modern city is nothing more than an incongruous salad, a hodge-podge of gross ugliness and blatant stupidity where glass beer halls contend with concrete chalets in a putrid barbarism not unlike the archaeological remnants of an ancient muscovite outhouse. Decisions are made by people with as little taste as intelligence and the patrons of the arts are cliques of men in suits and ties, bands of brigands who briefly pause from selling washing machines and circuit boards in order to piss out their inadequate millions on giant gypsum board barns. The intelligent man has no choice but to either bury himself in some hole in a mountainside like the saints of old, or bandage his eyes with the numbing fumes of vodka and quietly await the apocalypse when the earth will be cleansed of all inequilibrium."

Peter was impressed. He gazed at Nachtman as one would a prophet, for the latter's words touched the inner being of the younger man.

"But there is still hope," he murmured, a hint of desperation apparent in his voice.

"Hope? When you speak of hope you might as well be speaking Eskimo."

"But good men . . . can build a better world."

"Maybe by stacking block-heads one atop the next. . . ."

"But the project—are you interested in submitting a design?"

"Me? What do you want with me? Why do you want *me* to submit a design? I am not, after all, either pinhead or worm, either sycophant or numbskull, and will not have either my person or intellectual property toyed with. My ambition is as tame as an old eunuch. Give me a patch of sunlight under which to sit, a piece of meat to eat and a bottle to drink, and I am content. What need have I to mix with the world and contend with younger men—cringing gigolos who would trade their pallid thighs for the merest hint of fame."

"I can promise you my full support. And my aunt, who is a member of the board, will be your advocate."

"It takes money to build."

"There is money—plenty of it!"

"And . . . I am wanted?"

"You are, um, expected."

"Well, if there is lots of money . . ."

IV.

The board waited in silence. The windows were open, letting in the warm spring air. Dr. Enheim stood silently beneath the portrait of Körn, occasionally running his fingers through his beard in a thoughtful manner. The others sat as still as statues.

"I don't like waiting for people," Enheim observed.

"Yes, they are late," Borromeo said, looking at his watch.

Maria: "Only ten minutes."

"Still, not a propitious beginning."

Presently, however, the architect did arrive. Accompanied by Peter, he entered into the room, pompously, a bundle of papers tucked under one arm.

Handshakes. Formalities. Uncertain glances wandering over Nachtman's grotesque form.

"You wish to submit a proposal?"

"I am willing to let you look at some plans I have drawn up."

Dr. Enheim nodded his head gravely; Nesler sneered; Maria smiled slightly; Nachtman spread his papers out on the table and waved his hand before them as words came marching from his mouth.

"The structure will be audacious, as brave as God himself, as lyrical as *Die Zauberflöte*, that greatest opera of Mozart. It will be poetry in stone, a symphony of wood and steel. The exterior will be violently coloured, embedded with painted glass and lit by interior search lights. The central dome will be higher than St. Peter's in Rome—a half-oval that will dwarf Brunelleschi's Florentine masterpiece, and represent the cosmic womb which spits forth all life."

His eyes became glazed over like those of a visionary. He uttered his words in the manner of one reciting holy scripture.

"I can promise you," he said, his voice erupting from the depths of his torso, "that this will be the greatest structure built in the post-Atlantean age! It will be a symbol of the liberated spirit, of mankind's final dominance, not only over nature, but over physicality itself."

His enthusiasm was apparently contagious, for the eyes of all present had grown wide. They were no longer looking at the hodge-podge of lines and paper before them, but a massive edifice rising out of their dreams—each one's spirit stimulated, inflated by a mirage of future glory, gilded and dripping with arabesques.

The architect, thrusting his fingers here and there like daggers, baring his teeth like an angry dog, held forth:

"First we need to level this mountain. We will create a flat plateau upon which the structure, the Meeting Place, will be built. For the entrance, I suggest a hyperbolic paraboloid, and the interior will be a combination of upside-down and right-side up arches. The entire building, upon completion, will be 159 meters long and 119 wide and will mirror the cosmos, not only for its profundity, but also because it will be a harmonious system, modelled to some degree on the ideas of Petrus Apianus—a gemstone with the wings of a dragon, an ocean wave kissed by the moon."

And in long phrases piled one atop the next the architect set forward his scheme. He spoke of a building of great spiritual depth, of a place as wonderful as anything ever created by man and indeed which might more justly have been compared to some natural *theamata*, such as are found in the deserts of Utah or the depths of Australia—a thing that would easily rival the wonders of the ancient world and attract gods as readily as men.

"But this would take centuries to build!" Nesler objected.

"For an ordinary man, yes. But, fortunately enough, you are not dealing with an ordinary man. I propose to have the structure completed in four years time."

"That is not long," Borromeo commented.

"I have known postcards that have taken longer to be written," Maria said.

Nesler threw his hands up in the air, like a man half defeated, and it was indeed clear that, as extravagant as had been the architect's claims, his audience was not entirely ill-disposed towards his plan. For though the thin gentleman whose hands were lost in the cuffs of his shirt objected, the others gazed at the plans with dreamy eyes and seemed to be imagining themselves already strolling through its vast interior, hearing the voice of Körn echoing through its halls.

"Mr. Nachtman," Dr. Enheim said gravely. "Your presentation has been undoubtedly interesting. Of course we will need to deliberate this matter amongst ourselves."

"As you wish. I can go for a drink and come back in half an hour."

"Normally the decision-making process takes weeks if not months."

"That is all very well. It is the same to me whether you hire me or not. For I must tell you that there are others currently seeking my service and, naturally, I work on a first come first serve basis."

"Naturally."

"And it is spring. If you expect me to get started this year, you had better give me a definite answer—today if possible."

"Let him come back in an hour," Maria said, "we can surely tell him something by then."

And so it was that the architect and the young man found themselves at a nearby bar, awaiting a word from the board.

Nachtman ordered a beer, Peter an espresso .

"My aunt was very impressed. I could tell."

"Your aunt, young man, is a minotaur in skirts."

"She is a remarkable woman."

"Hell, in the end women are all the same. Pretty, ugly, intelligent or idiot. Good for one thing." He took a swallow of his drink. "For a hundred and fifty francs . . ."

"What?"

"You can get yourself the best of them."

Dr. Enheim stood behind his beard, one hand stretched before him dramatically.

"Mr. Nachtman" the man said gravely. "The Society has decided to accept your proposal. You will build the Meeting Place!"

"I will need money."

"You will have it."

"And full, undiluted authority concerning both the architectural and engineering aspects of the project."

"It shall be as you wish. But . . ."

"Yes?"

"Mr. Nachtman, are you a member of the Society?"

"I am not."

"The one stipulation we have, is that you become a member."

"And what do I need to do that?"

"Initiation and payment of member dues, five-hundred Swiss francs annually. . . . Naturally, the latter could be deducted from your pay."

"And what is my pay?"

"The pre-determined sum is seventeen thousand francs a month throughout the duration of the project and an additional four-hundred thousand upon its successful completion."

"Then initiate me, by all means," the architect said, with a sudden unpleasant obsequious note in his voice.

V.

Nachtman's past was clouded in obscurity, was like some tattered document, illegible in places, with bits torn off—dog-eared and smelling faintly of the sewer.

Some facts, however, were clear, from phrases the man himself had uttered, from comments Peter heard made by others.[1]

He had been born in a small village near the Swiss-German border. His father had been a civil servant who collected books. As a child, he had been very manual and enjoyed working with wood. In school he received poor grades, which seemed due to laziness rather than a lack of intelligence. At a young age he was apprenticed to a neo-functionalist furniture maker in Bern

[1] A teacher at the architectural school in Mendrisio, who had studied with Nachtman at the Stuttgart University of Applied Sciences: "I remember him. He was a very good-looking young man. I have no doubt that he won the hearts of many ladies. He was the sort of fellow one both admired and hated. . . . I lost track of him completely. Then, years later, I saw him again. I did not recognize him at first. He was overweight and had lost most of his hair. Undoubtedly he had been living a life of recklessness and debauchery. I talked to him. He was haughtier than ever. His views were far too anarchistic and dark for me. I had no desire to renew my acquaintance and, pleading a pressing appointment, wished him a good day."

and, wandering beneath the chilly arcades, influenced jointly by the fine old buildings around him and the modern work he was being trained in, he let his mind plummet into the past while carrying with it bomb-like fantasies of the future.

- He became further interested in architecture after reading Hermann Muthesius's Das Englische Haus.
- He began making little models of buildings out of scraps of wood—beautiful towers, castles with egg-shaped turrets.
- A rich man saw his work and supplied him with a grant to go to school and he went on to study architecture at the Stuttgart University of Applied Sciences.

In school, instead of basing his designs on standard geometrical shapes, he often imitated the shapes of plants and animals—of flowers and birds, studying nature's angles and curves and transposing them onto buildings—towers which rose up like giant mushrooms, housing complexes in the shape of bee-hives. Places that looked as if they had been shaped by wind and waves. Public buildings without doors and houses that were like labyrinths with hallways like intertwined ribbons. He dreamed of building hyperboloid places, hallucinogenic structures, towers which dived down into the earth and crypts which rose into the air, integrating the fluidity of water into his designs and energetically studying catenary principles.

Stimulating his young brain with glasses of schnapps, he snatched inspiration from the recesses of his soul and laboured to transfer these chimeras to paper. He read a great deal, devouring everything from the best-known works to the most obscure, everything from Pugin's *Chancel Screens and Rood Lofts* to Shen Kuo's *Dream Pool Essays.*

His peers, for the most part, hated him, as mediocrity hates genius. His designs were laughed at and scorned, making lips curl in disdain and drawing forth blunt insults from the mouths of those young scholars who in general could not see their value and were glad to make them a running joke around the school. Others, the more intelligent, could well perceive their merit, but ridiculed them all the same—out of jealousy and fear. They considered him perverse and took whatever opportunities they could to slander him and he, hypersensitive to criticism, rebelled and let invectives pour from his mouth like filth from an overflowing sewer. As he had no friends at school, he made them at the local bars—drunken old men, women of pornographic virtue, thieves and brutish labourers who shared with him their vices, as some saints might their crusts of bread.

He could well enough have got on without the love of his fellow students, but difficult indeed is it to be despised by one's teachers.

One day, near the end of his second term, he submitted a series of designs to his professors—ideas he had developed through long meditation—through sleepless nights and potions of liqueurs. There was an apartment complex shaped like an amoeba, a house in the shape of a blade of grass, and an office complex shaped like a pebble. This adoption of biomorphic forms won him no sympathy from his teachers. They felt affronted, challenged—and the young man's attitude did little to cure them of this impression.

"These ideas are the most original," Nachtman said.

"Somehow they strike me as being vaguely communist," one teacher commented.

"Black anarchist is more like it," another growled.

From that time forward he was looked on with great suspicion, and the professors themselves were glad to expose him to the taunts of his comrades, happy to try any means to defend and preserve their linear ideas.

It was indeed with great wonder that young Nachtman one day saw a shopping centre rising up at the edge of town that strongly resembled his amoeba plan. Upon enquiring who the architect was, he was surprised to learn that it was none other than Herr Schlindt himself, the very teacher who had derided his idea.

Propelled by feelings of anger and rebellion, he finally left school and, armed with abstraction, went out into the world, into the deep forests of concrete and across the deserts of asphalt. He expected to be received as a genius, to be at long last recognised as a true artist, but the doors he knocked at would not open, those he met were without faces—without speech and their cold skin let off the subtle resonance of capitalist horrors.

Nachtman was eloquent. But his eloquence was of that fiery type more suited to a prophet than a man in search of work. Riches are built of whispers, poverty of shouts—shouts which remind people of discontent, make them clutch their wallets nervously and avoid ill-lit streets.

No one was interested in his designs for giant inflatable buildings and only a few blind men, walking with canes, would bother gazing at his plans for subterranean housing complexes.

Truth be told, if we look at the lives of successful contemporary architects, it will be difficult to find a single one who is not an *arrivista*, a social climber. Enormous sums of money are spent on buildings. More often than not projects are consigned according to cronyism rather than merit. Blasé boxes are draped in the uncertain language of art and it often seems as if the entire world has fallen asleep beneath a perforated steel canopy—drugged by imbecility and a sick sense of utility—which is in fact nothing more than a useless attempt to pack an endless void with specks of dust.

- He wrote a short manifesto called Crimes and Barbarisms, a scathing criticism of his contemporaries which won him many enemies, but no fame.

- He had odd jobs: as a land surveyor, a draughtsman, a carpenter, but he could never hold on to work. Convinced of his own mental superiority, he was incapable of being a subordinate to men of modest intelligence. Having been blackballed from one profession after another, he was forced to assume pseudonyms to earn a living. Under the name of Max Costa he assisted Böhm on the Züblin Office Building. As Ludwig Mayner he worked with Makovecz on the Sárospatak Cultural Centre.

- Under the name "The Mole" he submitted designs to several important contests, and even was presented as a finalist for the International Architecture Decathalon. But when people saw who he was, saw him standing before them, arrogant and smelling of strong spirits, they quickly excluded him.

- Later, he worked as a stage designer, painter and etcher. He briefly went in for underwater photography and spent several years as a short order cook at a restaurant that specialized in fried foods.
- It had been rumoured that, through a number of different women stationed in various corners of Europe, he had fathered dozens of children, none of which he was willing to acknowledge.

VI.

Due to the fact that several influential politicians were members of the Society, the summit of Mt. Generoso had been acquired for a building site.

The mountaintop was at 1,700 meters. To the south one could make out Milan, Italy, and on a clear day the Duomo of its central piazza glittering in the sun. To the north, Mt. Blanc—the fabulous Alps. From the peak, looking down, the lakes of Como and Lugano could be seen. A cluster of tall pines grew along one side of the ridge, while the other was bare. A narrow-gauge cogwheel train connected the summit to the nearby towns.

The south side of the mountain was overgrown with rich heather and touched with wild peonies, white asphodel and red lilies. Narcissus grew from dense grasses and narrow-leaved hellebore opened their eyes. The rich smell of goat droppings perfumed the air and the cry of the goat herders was often heard, whooping and lonely. There were chamois which sprang away at the approach of men and occasionally a bird of prey circled overhead.

The mountain was dotted with *bolle*—cisterns of slate to catch the falling rain water for the goats and sheep. Paths led up from the villages below and the place was frequented by hikers who wore shorts and broad-brimmed hats and sometimes, when the weather was especially nice, women from

Como and Milan would appear and sunbathe right there on the slopes amidst the heather and dung, their eyes concealed behind sunglasses, their backs glistening with coconut oil.

The goat bells, however, were soon drowned out by the clang of machinery and those people who came there for leisure driven away by the guttural shouts of working men. Trees were cut down wholesale, trunks uprooted. Through ample use of dynamite, the top of the mountain was levelled into a flat plateau. Bulldozers carved a road in the side of the remaining elevation, so a continuous line of trucks could haul away the debris. Huge cranes extended themselves into the air, jack-hammers ripped away at rock and the groan of steel competed with the high-pitched whine of saws.

The mountaintop became littered with shirtless workmen, some with cigarettes dangling from their mouths, others bent over, their hairy backs resembling those of bears—warriors of the construction industry who thrust out their chests and formidable bellies, talking in exaggeratedly loud voices, spitting out humorous one-liners and peppering their speech with invectives. Many wore bright orange trousers, while the only clothing for others was a pair of shorts and heavy, steel-toed boots.

For the most part, the work force was made up of Italians and Swiss-Italians. At lunchtime they would lounge about on the south slope of the mountain, on the grass, eating sandwiches, drinking bottles of cheap Merlot, subdued noise trickling out through small hand-held radios. When they spoke, they moved their words about like bricks, using short, muscular phrases which fell to the earth rather than took to the wind.

"A nice place to work."

"Not bad."

"*Porco cane!* Wait till winter comes."

"Money's always money."

"If you don't have to pay to earn."

"Pass the salami."

"A handful of corn . . ."

"Anyhow, you aren't getting paid to be at Play Motel."

"Pass the red."

"*Caspita*, you drink, don't you?"

"Miracle water."

"Soap water . . . "

". . . and other beverages."

Just then the foreman approached, signalling them back to work with a motion of his hand.

This man, Fabrizio Fabrizi by name, was an Italian around forty or forty-five years of age, with blond hair and a handsome, neatly-trimmed moustache resting beneath a rather prominent nose. He had a cleft chin and a broad chest and went about in button-up shirts, with the sleeves rolled up, and blue jeans. He had worked on many large projects and had the commanding presence necessary to make the formidable men in employ do what he wanted without needing to waste too much breath.

There was an air of excitement about the site, a constant coming and going of people, movement of materials, and machines of every description. Forklifts which stuck their fangs into pallets of materials, tractors which ripped at the hard surface of the earth, and hydraulic excavators which crawled along it, waving their booms and buckets. Men hugged jackhammers and let themselves be swallowed into the cabs of great trucks whose formidable knobbed tires crushed all in their paths, and whose exhaust pipes coughed up clouds of black smoke. There were huge bulldozers and aerial work platforms, pile drivers with diesel hammers and an enormous drilling machine whose bit was like some fantastic upside-down minaret. Graders worked at flattening the mountain, while grapple skidders did away with trees. A giant crane had been ordered for when the structure would begin to mount its way to the heavens.

Nachtman, wearing a white jacket and white pants, the legs of which were tucked into a pair of brown leather boots, strode about the building site, his large head covered by a pith helmet, a steady stream of orders flowing from his lips. Eyes glazed, body fuelled by alcoholic spirits, he worked tirelessly; thundered, chased his belly from one end of the site to the other, ejaculating orders, energising the work force and maintaining the strictest discipline, demanding militaristic punctuality from them.

Peter, who had been hired on as the great man's assistant, worked conscientiously—copying out diagrams, as well as doing some microlevel planning. He did meticulous calculations and, when not glued to his desk, could be seen on the site, looking through the eyepiece of a theodolite.

On one such occasion, one warm day, made especially pleasant by a very slight breeze which blew from the east, he was doing just that, when Borromeo approached him. The latter had ridden his mountain bike up to have a look around, and his muscular thighs were invested in spandex shorts.

"Ah, it's really invigorating up here!" the athlete said.

"Yes, it is a beautiful spot for a building."

"And how are things getting on?"

"Excellently. Things are going far more quickly than anyone could have hoped."

They did not speak for a moment as Borromeo took in the view and Peter continued his operation, measuring out distances and taking notes on a small yellow pad of paper.

Presently he stopped his work and looked up. On the opposite side of the site he saw Enheim, who was walking with a young lady of around twenty or twenty-two attached to one arm, and with the other was making broad gestures, clearly showing her the works.

Borromeo, following Peter's gaze, explained:

"That is his daughter."

"I didn't realise he was married."

"He isn't. But she's his daughter all the same. Born out of wedlock I believe. A Hungarian woman who later killed herself in a tragic manner."

"Ah!"

"And the daughter lives with Dr. Enheim, who has brought her up. Her name is Trudy."

Peter repeated the name under his breath and watched as the figure made her way across the piles of torn up earth, stepping carefully, lifting her dress slightly so that it would not get dirtied, showing an extremely white strip of calf.

When, a quarter of an hour later, he was introduced to the young lady, he held his own heart in his hands.

She was rather short, slightly plump and had a shy demeanour—and indeed it was apparent that she had been raised on the rich cooking of Enheim's kitchen, where butter was used in abundance and a meal was never complete without a dessert of a few cheeses. Her eyes, which were large and dark brown, not unlike those of a young cow, fascinated Peter.

"This is a girl I would like to know better," he thought.

1. Monopan
2. Tinted concrete
3. Grey glass
4. Bituminous fibreboard
5. Weathered brass
6. Perforated steel
7. Mastic asphalt

VII.

The apartment of Maria Venezuela in Lugano was a model of elegant simplicity. A series of large, plate-glass windows gave a lovely view of the lake. A Tibetan tanka on one wall, a Russian icon on another. An Iranian felt rug partially covered the parquet floor in the living room. Furniture: a glass-topped table and a black leather couch. Huge cushions on which one could sit. Her mantle was covered with bric-a-brac—small Indian idols—a few grotesque Chinese figurines.

The dining room had a vaguely oriental feel to it. The table and chairs spoke elegant simplicity. The only decoration was an antique print of chrysanthemums which gazed on Maria placidly as she opened a bottle of organic French wine. She clicked glasses with her nephew. The table was laid: salad, whole-wheat pasta with wild Norwegian salmon sauce.

Peter twisted some noodles around his fork.

"Things are going marvellously," he said. "It is really quite incredible to see the speed at which he works. He is indefatigable. And it is not as if he is a young man!"

"He is fuelled by his dreams."

"Oh, I don't know about that. To me he simply seems like a man who is very true to himself. He looks towards the end result and is not concerned with money or fame. He has not sold out his ideals."

"It seems that he has found at least one disciple."

Her nephew shrugged his shoulders. "And what is wrong with that? I can learn a great deal from him."

"Yes, but . . . there is something about him that . . ."

"That what?"

Maria had become quite serious. A vague, indefinite smile flitted across her lips.

"Well," she said, "there is something about him that frightens me."

"You must be joking!"

"No. I don't mean that I find him frightening in the way one would some sort of monster. . . . No, it is more like standing on the edge of an abyss. I wonder sometimes if his plan is not too—ambitious!"

"It is ambitious, there is no question about it. But, it is not *too* ambitious. After all, people surely said the same thing about those ancient architects who designed the great pyramid—and yet now it is the only wonder of the ancient world still standing."

The two ate together in silence for some minutes. And then, as Maria was serving the salad, Peter said: "Well, I hope you have not lost any of your enthusiasm for the project."

"On the contrary. I am more enthusiastic than ever. Having a great meeting place, a place where members of our society from the four corners of the earth can come and learn in a spiritual environment, is truly of the highest importance to me. And I cannot deny that Herr Nachtman is a man . . . with certain merits."

"Yes, he is."

"I believe in this project because it will benefit humanity."

Peter was unsure of this, but kept his opinion to himself. He did not put a great deal of importance in *humanity* but did consider architecture to be the ultimate expression of the human will. Humans for him were, after all, only great because of their ability to shelter themselves—to, with earth and stone, recreate the world, chisel beauty out of its sulking form—wipe away forests and replace them with cities, drain away swamps and lagoons, where only eels and weeds prospered, so that man and woman could have mazes in which to live, love, hate and murder—play out their dramas.

"I certainly hope it will succeed," he limited himself to saying.

"Of course it will. As long as Nachtman is not a charlatan."

"And he is not!"

"Yes, if we trust our presentiments . . ."

VIII.

A golden dust filled the air. Piles of building materials were stacked everywhere. Helicopters whirred overhead, dropping loads onto the plateau from the ends of ropes and trucks and freight cars crawled up the side of the mountain, all adding to the constant flux of activity, adding to that aura of exhilaration which was crowned by a rainbow of quarried rock.

The architect ordered supplies in abundance, all of the highest quality, huge quantities of marble, imported from Italy, Spain and Greece, which piled up, creating geometric fortresses: some blocks were silky white in colour, while others were black as night. There was Carrara white, Prato green, and red from Siena. There were blues, which resembled a spotless sky at dusk and cream-coloured blocks from Sicily. Pinkish marble from Valencia, which was veined with red, giving it the look of unhealthy, naked flesh, complimented dark, blood-coloured reds from Alicante which resembled cubes of raw meat. And then other stones, a magnificent assembly which crowded in from all sides: Mesozoic red sandstone from Utah and old red sandstone from Scotland. From Northern Italy he had ammonitic limestone brought in and from Wisconsin beautiful ordovician dolostone, with subtle green tints—hints of pine, the freshness of damp moss. There were chert nodules from England, quaternary breccia from Austria and ignimbrite from New Zealand and walking among these stacks of stone was like walking through some treasure chamber laden with the most precious gems—for they carried with them qualities of the exotic, some seeming as soft and colourful as parrot feathers, some as weighty and rich as gold or platinum. Lace-like aquamarine snowflakes and stones which seemed like goblets of wine.

One day Nesler visited him in his tent.

"I have been receiving some rather extraordinary bills," he said.

"Yes, I have had to order a great deal of materials."

"That is evident. But is it really necessary to have boatloads of stone brought over from the United States and New Zealand?"

"It is."

"And why, might I ask, are such expensive products needed, when there are, as far as I can understand, products equally suitable, and far cheaper, near at hand?"

"Because, my dear fellow," the architect said raising his eyebrows, "these stones each have certain qualities that are irreplaceable. The ignimbrite from Hinuera, for example, is a truly exquisite volcanic pyroclastic rock with pinkish-grey tones. And I believe no other would do for cladding the walls of the Temple of Nesler."

"The temple of . . . ?"

"The Temple of Nesler, which will be a mid-sized chapel on the east side of the structure. A temple of algebraic intensity which will carry your fame five-thousand years into the future."

"An interesting idea . . ."

IX.

Earth had been excavated, the foundations laid, and now the walls, great hedges of stone, were being built across that expanse kissed by the clouds.

Gradually a structure began to rise up, stone by stone—to push itself up from the mud of the earth to the blue of the sky. It was like some great mushroom, seemingly swelling up out of nothingness amidst a network of scaffolding. Each day more work was done and that giant stone foetus stretched itself forth, like the golem created by Elijah Ba'al Shem, which grew ever bigger. Nachtman, by sheer willpower, seemed to be dragging it out of the mountain, to be giving life to inanimate materials—like a magician casting his spell over clay. The men obeyed his sometimes frantic gestures and occasional screams, though the effect of his madness was somewhat mitigated by the foreman who acted as a breakwater between this fanatic of architecture and his workers.

And though, as a rule, construction is the most dangerous of occupations, this project proved to be considerably more dangerous than most.

The position of the structure was such that, more often than not, a slight mistake would mean sure death—for to one side there was a sheer drop of a good three or four hundred meters, and strong winds often came about, making balance difficult. Occasionally a worker, losing his footing, would fall from the heights of that vast structure and be broken to bits on the rocks below or find himself unpleasantly skewered by a tree.

Then there were the stones themselves, which Nachtman, obsessed with the gigantic, insisted on having cut into as large of units as possible, so that, if these were mismanaged, they proved exceedingly dangerous, and on more than one occasion some poor fellow had his leg crushed or was bodily buried beneath one.

But such was the grandeur of the project that these contra-temps went by all but unnoticed. A helicopter would come to remove the corpse and a quarter of an hour later the work force would be at it again at full throttle, throwing up stone and scaling ladders and, indeed, their sheer numbers made the losses seem but a trifle, like a great army having a man occasionally break away from its ranks.

The sound of drills filled the air[1] like the sound of war; the mountain itself had been decapitated like some traitor—to be mounted with a new head of stone. And Peter, gazing through the little windows of glass mounted before his eyes, resting on his long nose, looked on at the assault wave of shirtless men going about their work, bouquets of stout individuals pounding away at concept to make it reality. Obedient to their foreman, they attacked in squads, striking with their hammers and kicking with their boots. Some held grinders or impact wrenches in their hands and all went about with helmets, lending the scene a decidedly military aspect.

1 gggggggggggggggggggggggggggggggggggggggggggggggggggggggggggggggggg

The young man's lips curled into something loosely resembling a smile as he took note of the great progress that had been done in such a short period of time and then, seeing Fabrizio approaching his person, his mouth returned to its usual austere pastures, where it grazed momentarily on his tongue as his hand pushed the wings of his hair back away from his eyes.

"The work is getting on well," he commented.

"Yes."

"You don't seem very satisfied."

"I am satisfied with my crew, but . . ."

"Well?"

"They do what they're told. The building is going up."

"Yes, the building is going up, and much faster than most of us expected. So what's the problem?"

"Nachtman."

"Is a great architect."

"That may be. But he's not a structural engineer and hasn't brought in one to help him. It seems to me that he has also been careless about the geotechnical aspects of the project, without paying proper attention to the soil mechanics of this mountain—the seepage, the best possible ground, rock anchors and so forth."

"I have faith in him," Peter said defensively.

"That's fine," the other replied with a rather cold grin, showing a mouthful of healthy white teeth. "But making a building shouldn't require faith, but simply science. Many of the ideas he is basing this project on went out of date five-hundred years ago, and the more modern elements he is using he doesn't seem to fully understand."

"I fundamentally and respectfully disagree with you, but can see how his ideas might be somewhat beyond your level of comprehension. After all, he is an architect and you are simply a foreman. I am dedicated to Herr Nachtman, so you had better keep these negative thoughts to yourself."

With these words Peter walked off, was soon on the north side, where the wind flowed through his hair, where workers looked at him with scepticism as they went about their tasks.

He came across Enheim questioning one of them, waving his arms about vehemently. The former, catching sight of Peter, approached.

"Where is he?"

"Who?"

"Herr Nachtman of course."

"In his tent no doubt."

"No doubt," the other said with agitation, striding off without offering further explanation.

A few minutes later he did find the architect in his tent, sitting with papers, plans spread before him, a mug of beer at his side.

"Ah, my dear Enheim, please come in."

The other sat down opposite. He wore a concerned look on his face and his beard drooped gravely over his chest. After running his hand over this great object, as if to calm it, as if he were petting an angry bull, he began.

"I have been looking over the site."

"And I hope that you like what you see."

"It would be impossible to deny that the work is phenomenal and is proceeding at an exquisite pace, but . . ."

"Please continue."

"The structure that you are building."

"Yes?"

"It seems to be considerably larger than that originally proposed."

"It is. Very much larger."

"Before making changes, particularly such important ones, you should have consulted the board. It is far from impossible that we would have had reservations about the enlargement of the scheme."

"This is art, my friend. I cannot go running off every time I have a fresh inspiration and have matters be decided by committee."

"But this is a significant change, and now that it has been done, retrogression seems impossible!"

"And so it is. We cannot go back, only forward. We can only march on. But have no fear, for your building is going to be the grandest on the face of the earth—the envy of nations—a structure to rival the pyramids of old. But you must understand that, for it to be so, I must be left in complete control. All great decisions are made by one man alone—they are not done on an assembly line. If Alexander had had to consult a committee . . ."

"Yes, yes, I see your point. But undoubtedly, following your new scheme, extra expenses will be incurred."

The architect shrugged his shoulders.

"Nesler is in charge of accounts. I only know that I will finish what I have begun."

X.

It was one of the better restaurants in Lugano and they sat one across from the other, a small plate of pâté de foie gras in front of each.

The women in the place were elegant; the men those staid fellows who spent their lives heroically plundering the earth of its treasures while cultivating broad moustaches to hide the greedy twitching of their lips or, the keener among them, freezing their faces with Botox so they might lie with greater ease. And while their bank accounts were puffing themselves up with interest, while the stock exchange was magically endowing these idiots with wealth, their lisping mouths habituated to gasping out the thin frail phrases of a decayed, practically stillborn century, gobbled up all the expensive trash they could—from awful steaks suffocated in sauces, asphyxiated in butter and staggering with sherry, to desserts that would make an honest man vomit, so rich they were, glutted with cream and liqueur.

Dr. Enheim took a sip of white wine. His grave face wore a look of preoccupation as he applied his knife to the pâté before him and spread it on a small piece of toasted white bread.

- His formidable belly rested on his thighs.
- The fattened livers of force-fed geese screamed.
- Taste buds whipped them with vines.

"You don't seem in the best of spirits," Maria commented.

"Yes, I am preoccupied. I want to speak to you about Nachtman."

She frowned.

"Do you want to speak, or to lecture?"

"Please, do not be harsh with me. There was a time when you greatly enjoyed my lectures."

"And I still do. In the proper context."

"Nachtman, he seems to be having a somewhat contrary effect on the Society. He is too headstrong. What was meant to be a simple architectural project for the betterment of mankind is turning into our central focus. I fear that, from the spiritual point of view, we might have chosen the wrong man."

"Are you sure that your concerns truly rest with Nachtman's effect on the Society and not the damage it has done to your own ego? Because some attention has been taken away from you, you say that this is bad for the Society. Is the Society then just another Caesaristic institution? I can hardly believe it! If Dr. Körn were alive today, he would be thrilled with the work Herr Nachtman is doing. I feel, quite strongly, that the construction of the Meeting Place has raised the consciousness of all of our members. Do you not feel, as I do, that he is imbuing the very blocks of stone which make up the structure with the essence of the divine? Is there not something occult in the work he has done?"

"I am not saying there is not. . . . But centralisation of power . . ."

"What vanity!"

"Then you honestly believe that I am speaking out of mere egotism?"

"Yes. You are acting like a chimpanzee. Some poor man suffering from testosterone poisoning. It is a classic example of inter-male aggression."

The doctor stuffed a piece of bread in his mouth with embarrassment.

Maria, leaning forward, put her hand on his arm.

"Herman," she said, "are you being honest with yourself?"

Enheim bowed his head.

"Surely," she continued, "this cosmos is big enough for more than one great man."

It was at that moment that the waiter, a short individual resembling to a remarkable degree an aged Buster Keaton, brought them their second course, i.e. thigh of capon beneath a cream and herb sauce. Dr. Enheim gravely began to eat it as if he were eating his own guts.

After the meal, Maria, who needed to give a ylang-ylang treatment to a prominent auto manufacturer from Milan, took her leave of the doctor and he strolled along one of the main thoroughfares, and then to the park, letting his digestion do its work, thinking over their conversation.

"That man is undermining me," he thought. "As ugly as he is, he still seems to fascinate, to have some arcane variety of charisma which enchants the less wise. I fear indeed that he will bring ignominy on the Society."

Ducks swam in the lake and boats floated. The grass was a bright emerald green. The trees stretched out their branches dramatically and beneath one some men sat, drinking large bottles of beer.

The doctor knew a good many people in the town and nodded to these as he walked along, casting glances of recognition at old women whose fingers slumped under enormous diamond rings and young suited men with gorged wallets bulging from their back pockets.

One gentleman, around forty-five years of age, short and slightly balding, with a thick moustache and glasses, stopped.

"Ah, Dr. Enheim, so nice to see you!" he said, grasping the hand of the Commander Adeptus Magus.

"Signor Uccellini."

This was Signor Pietro Uccellini, member of the National Council in Bern, an elected representative of Canton Ticino.

He wore the broad, confident smile of the politician. A smile that had, just a few months previous, instilled so many voters with confidence, despite the fact that its proprietor was an acknowledged womanizer, a man who had been arrested for driving while intoxicated and was said to be a user of certain white powders. But only fools, radicals, those who have no confidence in democracy, judge a man by how he lives rather than by the fluidity of his speech and the precision with which he knots his tie.

"I was just up at the building site today, and I must say that I am very impressed. I cannot tell you how much I admire your courage for going through with such an ambitious project. It will no doubt bring great glory to our region and economic benefits in the form of tourism. Ah, a brilliant fellow that architect you have working for you! When you get finished with him up there on the mountain, we'll find some things for him to do down here, for there are still a great many old villas to tear down and replace with apartment complexes and lots of public funds which desperately need to be routed away from social services, from immigrant benefits and the like, into more useful channels, such as the building of new roads, parking lots and industrial piazzas."

"Yes, um, we will see this project through in the grandest style," Enheim said, flourishing his hand in an oratory manner.

After this brief encounter, he continued on his way.

"But maybe Herr Nachtman is not such a bad fellow to have as an ally," he thought.

XI.

Summer gave way to fall, to rain and denuded trees, and fall to winter—short days, and the equinox passed.

With limited daylight, the workers found themselves in the early evening working by the light of huge floodlights, their bodies casting bizarre shadows.

In the middle of January a huge storm came in. Mounds of snow fell from the sky. Down below, the cities were paralyzed. Trains did not move, cars did at their own peril. It was the heaviest snowfall in fifty years. Over 90 cm fell in 22 hours. Trees, heavy with snow, collapsed across roads and railroad tracks, impeding movement. Though it was almost impossible to get materials to the site, Nachtman still insisted that the men continue to work.

Dispirited, wrapped in huge coats, they went about their business—clearing the construction site of snow, building fires to keep the mortar from freezing. No longer did they sing and show their naked chests and at lunch it was not wine they drank, but hot broth which they chased down with abundant brandy. They smoked continuously, seeming to fancy that those tiny cherries, those cigarettes that they held between stiff, trembling fingers, would keep them warm. And, indeed, their hands were so cold that they could barely clutch their tools and the rock they chipped away at seemed as if it were great blocks of ice, it seemed as if they were building an enormous igloo for the worship of some Inuit deity of cold weather systems.

And for those who had to work on the western side of the structure it was even worse. A freezing cold wind came incessantly with such force that it could easily sweep a man away, make him lose his balance and send him spiralling off the cliff.

"If you lose your life, it doesn't matter how much they pay you."

"I'm already giving my last blood."

"It's a dirty story."

"Yes, I'll be damned if I kill myself for a few thousand lousy francs a month."

And, as if in answer to these words, just then a man was seen slipping, falling off the building, being dashed against the rocks. He had slipped on some iced-over scaffolding.

Nachtman, in a pair of huge, fur-lined boots approached the foreman.

"The conditions are horrible," the latter said. "If we could halt work until early spring . . ."

"Impossible. The building must go up. We cannot stop work every time one of the men feels a little chilly."

"But the danger—another man has just fallen!"

"Well, that is something we can take care of in spring. In this weather his body will certainly be well preserved."

XII.

A wood stove dispensed heat throughout the tent. Herr Alexius Nachtman sat at a table, beneath the light of an electric lamp, refining certain details of his plan, altering a line, changing a measurement. To one side of his diagrams sat an ashtray, in which burned a cigarette. To the other, a half-empty bottle of beer.

He heard a scratching at his tent door, as if an animal wanted to be let in.

"Who is it?"

The flap was lifted. An exquisitely white face peered out from beneath an ermine hat and the luxuriant collar of a sable coat. It was Maria.

"Do you mind if I come in?"

"Are you here to disturb me?"

"I hope not. I am only here to talk to you."

"It is rather late."

"I was able to find my way in the dark."

He rose from his seat and advanced to greet her. His nose inhaled her perfume, sandalwood oil, as his hand shook hers.

"May I offer you something to drink?"

"Yes. A Scotch. Neat."

"You know how to drink!"

"When the weather is chilly. . . . But, it's cosy in here," she murmured, settling down in a chair near the stove. She watched the architect as he poured two drinks. "I always find it exquisite to sit by a warm fire when it is cold outside. It makes me feel very young and happy."

"Well, you are not old," he said, handing her a glass, a third full of gold-coloured whisky.

"But I am no longer young."

"It is a matter of perspective. From my point of view . . ."

"But you are a man in the prime of life!"

"I am not much under sixty. Of course, my virility is more intact than many much younger beasts."

"I believe that a man like you needs . . ."

"Yes, tell me what I need."

"I believe that a man like you must need a very strong woman."

"A strong woman. An oxymoron. I have yet to meet a strong man. Is there such a thing as a strong woman?"

"There is."

"And what would I do with her?"

"Anything you wanted."

The tone of her voice was so naked that her meaning could not be mistaken. Nachtman was not a shy man. He grinned. His maxillary canine teeth, capped with silver, let off a slight sparkle. His shadow stretched off to one side, a distorted mass. His face, in the rather weak light of the tent, appeared manifestly infernal. A huge nose that seemed in the process of being swallowed by a jutting bottom lip, below which rested a grotesque mound of chin and neck. Maria moved towards him.

"Come as close as you wish," he said boldly.

She mixed her lips with his, devoured his ugly face with kisses.

XIII.

The next morning he awoke rather late. He was alone.

"Ah, the little bird has flown back to her own nest."

He threw a few logs into the wood stove, which still had hot coals from the night before.

Then, after dousing his face with water, oiling his mouth with a coffee mixed with schnapps, he put on his boots and left his tent to look over the project. A fierce wind howled, blowing about the strands of hair that fringed his skull. Snow was piled up on all sides and, driven up against by the wind, let off wisps of crystal which swirled about. He trudged forward, his breath forming puffs of white vapour.

Surprised by the silence around him, he looked both right and left. No men clung to the sides of the structure. No hammers resounded. The machines lay dormant, their engines grown cold. The place was abandoned.

Two figures made their way towards him.

It was the foreman and Peter.

"They have left," Peter said gloomily.

"What's that?"

"Just like he said," Fabrizi added. "The work has ground to a halt. The men won't go on in these conditions. They say you need to raise their pay by at least forty percent if you expect them to continue through the winter. Otherwise they will be back towards the end of February, when the weather starts to warm up and the snow to melt."

"Why didn't you stop them?"

"Because I agree with them."

"Ah, now I see how things are," the architect said with an ugly twist of his lips.

An emergency meeting was called. The architect's tent was where it was held. The four board members were present, as was Peter and the foreman, who sat silently to one side—for he was there not so much to participate, as simply to answer any questions that might arise.

"The situation is serious," Nesler said. "These men want more money, but we are going to have a hard enough time maintaining the accounts due as it is. Materials have cost more than anticipated. Several of the Society's investments have recently proved the contrary of profitable. And now the workers want raises, but such a thing, from a financial point of view, is scarcely possible."

"Indeed it is," Nachtman added. "And these lunkheads who spend more time scratching their bellies and smoking cigarettes than labouring should not only accept their current wages, but should do so gratefully, for in all truth a wage reduction seems far more in order than a rise."

"Yes," Maria agreed, "they should be penalised."

"They are men," Fabrizi could not help but putting in, "not beasts. They have families to support."

"Enough with the socialist clichés," cried the architect. "Such high-sounding phrases have no place in a convocation of intelligent men. . . . And while we are at it, I suppose you wouldn't mind an augmentation of your salary also, would you?"

The foreman rose to his feet.

"I do as my men do. If their salary is increased, so should mine be."

"You dog! You have scarcely got dirt under your fingernails these past nine months, and now you talk about additional money! Yes, you might be handsome, but that big square jaw of yours will get you nothing from me—from us. As it is you are only being kept on as a matter of charity—as a matter of formality, so that the great louts we have shovelling sand and chipping away at stone can have someone to lavish their idiocy on."

"I would recommend that you be quiet."

Nachtman bared his teeth.

"Quiet! I hardly need to be quiet before an inferior, a subordinate, a rebellious toady who knows as little about architecture as a——"

It was at that moment that his words were cut off by the fist of Fabrizio Fabrizi, a lump of bones and flesh which shot forward like a hand-drilling hammer striking at a masonry nail.

The older man lay sprawled on the ground, rubbing his jaw. Maria ran to him, kneeled down beside him, took up his hand and kissed it. Then, turning a flashing gaze on the handsome foreman, declared:

"Ah, you are really a very stupid person!"

"I defer to your judgement," the other said and then turned, left the tent with his head held high. And proudly he followed his golden moustache into the unknown and the valley below.

XIV.

The next day another meeting was convened in Lugano, at the offices of the Society. The portrait of Dr. Körn looked down. That man of paint seemed almost to be chuckling to himself, his eyes, magnetically moving spheres, inhabited by some dark angel, manipulating men from unseen planes.

All present were seated around the large, glossy oak table but Nachtman, who stood erect, proud, a band-aid plastered across his chin.

"We have a crisis on our hands," Dr. Enheim proclaimed.

"It is a problem, not a crisis."

"Yes, it is only a problem," Maria confirmed.

"We could still negotiate with the workers."

"No," said Nachtman. "That is out of the question. I will not tolerate those traitors on my work site."

"Cheaper labour must be found," Nesler said in a whiny voice. "We can no longer afford to pay outlandish prices for arms and legs."

"We could bring in Poles," Borromeo suggested. "I have heard that they work well for very little."

"I have nothing against Poles," Maria commented.

Nachtman waved the idea aside with a gesture.

"But why bring in Poles," he said, "when we have an untapped resource. After all, worldwide membership to the Society is formidable."

"I am not sure I follow you," Enheim said.

"The followers of Körn are all loyal citizens. Let them, with my guidance, build their own meeting place. Why rely on outsiders, who we must pay, to do what so many would be grateful to do voluntarily."

Nesler's little eyes gleamed. "You are right. We would save a great deal that way."

"But many of our members—the great majority—live abroad. Some in India. Others in China and Africa."

"Then let them come—from everywhere let them come!"

XV.

And so it was that disciples poured in from the four corners and eight directions of the Earth to lend their labour to the vast project. They arrived in great numbers, rolled up their sleeves, and set to work.

There were blonde-headed Swedes and dark-skinned Africans. Japanese stood beside Greeks and clean-shaven Russians laboured next to South Americans with silky black beards. A Ukrainian woman with a handkerchief tied around her head shovelled sand. An inadequately dressed young lady from California carried water. The people came, from north and south, from the mountains and the coast, uttering words in half the languages of the earth. The whole recalled some scene from the Old Testament—a vast undertaking such as might have been done by pharaohs of the Fourth Dynasty.

And it must be here said that the congregation were from all walks of life, from all strata of society. The rich, the educated, shoved themselves forward with as much vehemence as the illiterate, showing indeed that wisdom cannot be taught in schools and that the laws of social facilitation apply to all.

Businessmen unknotted their ties, slipped into overalls and let their soft hands, used to nothing heavier than banknotes, nothing harsher than the keys of a computer keyboard, make contact with abrasive work, while the lower classes lurched forward, calves taut, pulling at thick ropes, like donkeys or oxen. Lines of men, like tribes of ants, made their way about the structure, their backs bent under huge loads, the palms of their hands raw wounds from pushing against blocks of stone.

By the beginning of March they had ten thousand men assembled. By the middle of the same month, the number had more than doubled and by April there were no less than eighty thousand—enough to fill a small city.

The work force was divided into four gangs, named, respectively: the Friends of Körn, the Sons of Zeus, the Brothers of Julian the Apostate, and the Sisters of Future Well-being, the latter of which was put under the supervision of Maria. Each gang was then divided into five phyla of around five thousand workers respectively. With this huge, though admittedly rather unskilled work force, the building grew visibly day by day and seemed to be slowly revealing itself as if by magic—trembling in the light and sighing in the darkness; eating the rays of the sun and drinking in the moonshine. The walls wrapped themselves around the foundation and great pillars began to make their appearance, columns which stretched themselves out like fingers, seeming thereby to replicate the digits of the very hands that made them—those appendages of the ever-zealous Sons of Zeus, who indeed proved themselves to be the strongest, the most energetic of the phyla.

One of their number, an old Swedish man with a long white beard, went about his tasks with especial vigour. He had his feet eternally resting in a pair of hiking boots and liked to dress in polypropylene and polyurethane materials. He strained his thin arms, stuck forward his bird-like chest and worked in silence, rising well before dawn and not discontinuing his efforts until long after dark.

"Who is that fellow?" Nachtman enquired of Nesler.

"His name is Olaf Lidskog. He is an eccentric millionaire well dedicated to the cause."

"So he has donated?"

"Heavily."

There are few things in this world more frightening than voluntary slavery. The slave in shackles is without freedom, but has a will and hope, things which the voluntary slave has not. He has renounced the power to think for himself and without analytical thought, mankind would be nothing more than a hive of rather large insects—a horde of giant larvae feeding on every other living thing in their path. And yet there undoubtedly must be a certain kind of horrible peace in renouncing free-will, as the vast majority of human-kind is ready to do so, only needing to be asked by the right apostle.

Nachtman drove those disciples on with fiery words, kicks; hot exhalations of his stinking, liquor tainted breath, the pressure of his knuckle-studded fists. His voice, through almost constant yelling, grew hoarse and he seemed to be digging his words up from the depths of some horrible cave which respired sulphur and spat flames.

Dr. Enheim seemed determined to set an example and often arrived to lend his two hands to the great task. His labours were almost biblical in proportion. Stripped to the waist, sweat streaming down his face, he pushed along blocks of marble, with great burdens on his back climbed up the dizzying scaffolding like a baboon.

"If all of our workers were like him, the place would have been finished long ago," Nachtman commented.

He himself would not even pick up a hammer.

"Physical labour will drain my mental abilities," he said. "And God knows we need them."

XVI.

Aside from the work forces previously mentioned, there was another, an elite group called the Company of Good Men—a group hand-picked by Nachtman from the largest and most durable of the male devotees. Rivers of tendons and mountains of muscle. There was a fellow from Iceland with scant blond hair and a forlorn gaze who could pull along a tractor with his teeth and a pair of brothers from Pakistan with huge biceps who were able to play catch with enormous boulders. Men of maximised muscle. Men with predatory jaws. Columbians who could bend iron bars with their hands and Ukrainians who could jog about with 150 kg barrels under each arm.

Nachtman took these specimens, these already Herculean young men, and injected them daily with extract of dog testicles and anabolic steroids and kept them fed on abundant quantities of beef, chickens and baby food.

These men, who could each do the work of fifty, were the pride of the work site and seemed to vie with one another for performing incredible tasks. They dragged huge carts of gravel, were able to pound in nails with their bare palms, break up rock with their fists, and scale slick walls without the need of scaffolding or ropes. Their huge arms flung about blocks of stone, pulled them to the heights with pulleys and they worked almost without rest.

The architect took special care to make them his own, having them swear by secret oaths and their duties certainly went beyond that of mere workers, as they stood by ready to champion his cause, and even give their lives if need be.

"Master," Sergei from Russia said, "I am hungry."

"Ah, you boys eat so much. But I need to keep you healthy. A truckload of sheep has just come in for you and Pedro to unload."

And as the flowers of May shoved themselves up from the ground, those huge men shoved barely cooked and even raw flesh into their mouths, ravenously chewed on mutton.

XVII.

When Trudy visited the site, she was inevitably drawn to Peter. Their ages were similar. The one was the daughter of Dr. Herman Enheim, the other the nephew of Maria Venezuela. And they were both enthusiastic about this great undertaking. She always had a dozen questions regarding the project to ask him, and he was more than happy to have someone to listen to his voice.

And, gazing at her through his glasses, thrusting his long nose forward, he would wax eloquent, pouring forth his bizarre dreams of a future in which architecture was realised for what it was, the greatest of all arts, and nature was done away with, replaced entirely by buildings, cities—forests supplanted by well-planned gardens and oceans spanned by bridges.

She in turn, in a very quiet voice, casting shy gazes about, spoke enthusiastically about the Society, and about its great work, marching forward into a new spiritual age. She seemed to view things according to their transcendental qualities and her speech was always modified according to esoteric principles.

"Finally there will be a place where truth-seekers from all over the world can meet and learn in peace. This is true evolution. We will all be able to work together on a trans-dimensional level."

"You seem to know a great deal about the Philosophy," Peter commented.

She blushed.

"Yes, I try to put the etheric currents in my body to good use."

The young man, murmuring his approval, cast his eyes over her plump arms.

"And Herr Nachtman is fortunate to have you as his assistant, Peter."

"I am the one who is fortunate."

XVIII.

The power Nachtman had been given increased his personal sense of virility, to the joy of Maria, who worshipped, had indeed fallen deeply in love with him. She saw sunsets, white banks of clouds and green forests in his grotesque face. For her, the bark of his voice was as sweet as the song of birds and she wished to clothe him in pleasures. Tenderly she caressed the rough rind of his skin, joyfully offering him her most intimate treasures—her beryls and amber, her amethyst and topaz—performing nude snake dances before him, while to her right and left censors spilled out the smoke of spikenard and dried roses.

The psychology of love is infinitely complex;—female beetles are attracted to the ugliest males;—woman, primordial, is often suicidally drawn to the sharp horns and lances of the male and casts herself onto his personality like one hurling themselves from a cliff. A swirling sky; some cold and clumsy planet attracting a silvery moon. Black holes that gorge themselves on female energies and spit out nothing in return—the primitive writhing of the worm as it digs into some geological crack.

So Nachtman took her love as a matter of course.

She would arrive in his tent and, after rinsing his gums with schnapps, he would enwrap her in his arms and take her rapidly to the temple of debauchery, treating her to vulgarity sauced with plumeria and topinambur and he indeed seemed like the descendant of some ancient god or demi-god, some boar-headed divinity cast on earth in order to perform great deeds, to slaughter men and stack their corpses as high as the heavens, or a creature hatched from an egg, a man-lizard well versed in the obscene arts, which had fed itself for years on Indian and Mongolian love manuals and pickled itself in a cosmic vinegar of procreation. For, whatever one may think, it is often those old reptiles who know best which buttons to push, know how to poke amongst the springs and levers of love.

"You have given me life," she murmured.

"Lucky girl."

She lay her head on his chest.

"When I first saw you, I never imagined that this would happen."

"They never do."

And a long kiss, filthy and dark as a sewer, followed his words.

XIX.

The building site became imbued with an almost apostolic aura. In the evening, members of the work force would often perform some of the complex rituals prescribed by Dr. Körn—group meditations, initiations, cleanses and rites. Mystical texts were read aloud and songs were sung to the rattle of cymbals and the sound of the flute while special initiates revealed magical finger symbols. Dr. Enheim would ceremoniously rip the entrails from just-slaughtered cows and Maria, in a sweet high-pitched voice, chanted out the song of Isis while sugarcane and beans were distributed to her listeners.

These people, from diverse backgrounds and stations in life, felt a great sense of fraternity sitting together on that mountaintop amidst the blocks of stone and heavy machinery and, gazing into great bonfires, clasping each-other's hands, they felt indeed to be the chosen few. They were carried away by a sort of mass hysteria. Their one and joint desire was to see this grand structure transport them up to the skies and imbue their poor emaciated frames with immortality. It was a mass monomania, where the community, the Society, swallowed up all individual will, and, converted into a single superorganism, moved in concert. Their energies were channelled toward a single goal, which was to bring Nachtman's plan to completion and thereafter go to an eccentric universe where they would be born as sexless creatures of light with wings who would receive their nutriment directly from the atmosphere—a variety of moth much loved by the Great Creator who reclined placidly off in some vast and almost unreachable dimension, somewhat bored, while down below the fangs of men, upright wolves, dripped with blood and their claws greedily ripped the life from the very earth itself.

And so it is that the more desperate men become, the more wild are their dreams. Shunning the world around them, ignoring the blue skies and singing streams, they look for beauty in some great beyond, their diseased minds crippled by stupidity, their senses perverted by occult mechanisms.

Those workers, those devotees, suffered truly great hardships. They laboured fourteen hour days, seven days a week. Their diet consisted for the most part of thin soups and white bread. While working, the members were told to repeat mantra-like clichés to keep up their stamina and so there was a constant murmuring, like around a huge bee-hive.

The entire mountainside was crowded with tents. The number of people was more than it was possible to properly facilitate. They slept crowded one next to the other. Latrines were formed between the rocks and the people bathed in the unhealthy trickles of water which issued from between outcrops of mossy granite. Due to the unsanitary living conditions, many became ill, were seen vomiting in shrubs.

Dr. Enheim rallied the disciples, shook their hands, gave frequent speeches—giving them spiritual food in place of physical, talking about the comforts of other planes, where in some future time they would dine on the most exotic fruits and drink wine from the blossoms of flowers. They would write with solar beams rather than ink and harvest the energy of far away planets.

One evening, amongst the tents, before a great fire whose flames lurched towards the stars, a crowd of thousands gathered around him:

"In a time in which many are experiencing a crisis of spirit and search for meaning, we offer a chance to work and celebrate through service and community-building in which all participants flourish. We must gather together and oppose all selfishness!"

As he spoke, his voice grew more resonant, its rich tones flowing out over the multitude. He seemed a new Moses, who, with shittim wood in hand, pointed the way even beyond Horeb.

"With your hands, my friends, you are building a temple of universal brotherhood, where truth can be learned and spiritual endeavours nurtured. Let us sail together to this place, this future where the zodiacal constellations and five planets converge, and the Mysteries will be unveiled to all, in a context of light and friendship!"

There was a general sigh of approval. A teardrop rolled out of one woman's eye.

"I realise that much is being asked of you," the doctor continued, "but I also realise that, fortified by the wisdom of the great Maxwell Körn, you are up to the task. For from him we have learned that these bodies are not our true bodies, but only an illusion and we realise that our suffering and hardship are unreal."

It was well that the doctor spoke so, since suffering and hardship had most certainly become part of these disciples daily lot, dragging along Cyclopean blocks of stone, weighing as much as twenty tons each, mixing cold mortar before the sun rose and still finding themselves balanced at precarious heights when the moon came out. And yet, through it all, they were for the most part cheerful—for these were all people who had gone through years of thought reform, mystical manipulation which made them always put the Society first.

With glazed eyes and hungry bellies they listened to his words. Many were gladly willing to be devoured by the structure, to let it crunch their bones and chew off their heads. Many—but not all, for there were others, inspired by fear or some innate sense of self-preservation, who were not quite so keen.

A few whispered together, a few openly sneered—some wandered off into the darkness, cursing the mountain on which they stood.

XX.

Even though the group seemed to be compelled by some sort of mass hypnotism, madness, it was seen that the intensity of the labour soon caused infractions. Though minor at first—a man leaning on his shovel, a woman sitting down for a quarter of an hour to rest—a few more serious incidents soon occurred.

A young man from India complained rather too volubly about the living conditions saying that even on the streets of Calcutta one might do better—sleeping on the sidewalk with dogs and dining off nauseous waste. An Italian couple insisted on being fed better. An elderly gentleman from Morocco began to scream violently and declared that he would soon return home, even if he had to walk.

"We cannot let this sort of behaviour go unchecked," Nachtman said during the next board meeting. "Discipline is the key to the completion of the project. These workers are all we have. If they abandon us, the project is doomed."

"They will not abandon us," Dr. Enheim stated.

"No? Some of them are already beginning to murmur, a few to shout."

"But even if we lose a few people, I don't see how——"

"We cannot afford to lose anyone! If one goes, others will follow. The distance from a whisper to open rebellion can be covered in an instant and, as you well know, mankind is a gregarious animal and acts as a herd rather than as a group of individuals. Humans are like plagues of rats. They clew together, follow one upon the next like parcels of penguins. Furthermore," the architect added with a pompous wave of his hand, "Körn himself, in his Vienna lectures, said that educational discipline was the key to the betterment of mankind."

"What do you propose?"

"Well, there is obviously only one solution."

"Which is?"

"Corporal punishment. Severe corporal punishment for those who don't give themselves to us, from the ends of their toes to the follicles of their hair. Their very minds and individuality. Corporal punishment for those who don't conform to the requirements of the Society."

Borromeo smiled uneasily. "Don't you think that would be somewhat . . . brutal?"

"Come man! Do you think the pyramids would have ever been built without the help of the whip? In grand projects, the workers need whatever stimulation they can get. They should be shown what dedication means. It is simply a matter of healthy respect for authority. And I am quite sure, if Dr. Körn were with us today, he would agree with my point of view. After all, *He that spareth his rod hateth his son.*"

"But from a strictly spiritual perspective . . ."

"Aren't you listening to me? Am I shouting at walls? It is the spirit that I am concerned with. We must be willing to chastise the flesh if we hope to cleanse the soul. Only by suffering can these poor bastards hope to find the light!"

"I am afraid he is right," Maria said quietly. "These people need us. They need our guidance. We cannot be cowards. We are not doing them any favours by treating them so delicately. A small amount of hard-living will only help them"

Peter was dumbfounded.

"But what exactly are you planning on doing?" he asked.

"You will see," Nachtman said, standing erect and thrusting his index finger in the air like a spear. "Leave the matter in my hands and all will be well."

"You are the architect," Enheim pronounced gravely. "You are in charge of the project and of course must do what you think fit."

"Indeed he must," was Nesler's comment as he bobbed his head deferentially.

The next day the young and voluble man from India, he who had compared his sojourn in Switzerland disadvantageously to life in the streets of Calcutta, was busy smoothing the side of a giant block of marble. Nachtman, carrying in one hand a rattan cane, approached him.

"You have been refractory."

The other looked somewhat confused.

"I am not sure that I understand . . ."

"You have been belittling the community and disturbing their composure with your pusillanimous complaints."

"I am sorry about it."

"I am glad to hear that, my friend. But now, if you would be so kind as to step over here and touch your toes."

"My toes?"

"Touch them."

The man did as he was told.

The architect, majestically holding his head high, violently applied the stick to the other man's slim buttocks twelve times. With each stroke the poor fellow let out a painful cry. Afterwards, he was allowed to return to his work, which he went about with much vehemence.

Throughout the rest of the day the teams worked on in nervous silence, going about their business obediently, with heads hung low. Many felt inner joy at being part of something so great. Some felt fear and pressed their lips tightly together. Unfortunately, however, this was not the last disciplinary incident. Nachtman had his eye on several who he considered to be trouble-makers and infractions were not tolerated. Behaviour modifications were doled out to those who did not conform one-hundred percent to the requirements of the Society. These punishments were referred to as purges and were said to expel the demon of softness. Some were made to wear sackcloth and others, the more refractory, were smeared with honey and exposed to flies and wasps. Those who were caught uttering unflattering comments regarding either the project or the Society were made to wear branks—a bridle with a sharp iron to restrain the tongue. There were whippings and humiliations, cries which tore the calm of the mountain and tears of repentance.

And though in truth there were very few who had not consigned themselves body and soul to the project and fewer still who openly complained, the punishments gradually grew more severe. It being the nature of our species to be ever searching for new sensations, unlike bees who are satisfied with the dust of flowers, it came to pass that simple floggings no longer sufficed and the penalties became not so much a matter of discipline as being a demonstration of Nachtman's authority—a sacrifice to that man and to the great structure he was building, a thing which seemed to grow larger with every drop of blood spilt, a fungus that seemed to flourish in conditions of human suffering.

One day a young Spaniard was found asleep high up on a wall during working hours. It seemed probable that he had fallen asleep involuntarily, but the architect was still merciless.

"Shall we whip him?" Maria asked.

"No," was Nachtman's reply. "His crime is too severe for that. Cut off his leg."

And as it was said so it was done, the architect showing no particular signs of pleasure while meting out this chastisement, but also not showing the least repugnance.

XXI.

Mr. Daniel Nesler directed two organisations, the Körn Business Association (KBA), and the Association for Responsible Living (ARL), and with these was in charge of vast resources, gleaned from multiple sources—from investments to charity. From a unique line of herbal and homeopathic products to an arms manufacturer in Zürich—for the KBA was composed of 43 medium-sized businesses, all with their tax bases in Liechtenstein, which generated considerable wealth, while the ARL, though not involved in commerce, was still a formidable financial institution, as it took donations under a vast variety of headings. There were programs for feeding the hungry in Africa and for curing the blind in India. Conveniently, however, only a small amount of money given for these causes managed to find its way through the infinite maze of bank accounts and routing numbers, financial rubrics and Byzantine computations, to the place where it had been destined. The secret holdings in the banks of Switzerland and Nassau grew ever fatter, while a truly minute amount was dribbled into those needy Third World countries where it was gobbled up in an instant by blind beggars and weeping mothers, indigence opening its parched lips, displaying its decayed and unappealing mouth.

But, as wealthy as the Society was, it did not seem to be able to meet the needs of the structure. Huge sums had been spent on costly marble and exotic woods. Machinery had been purchased and millions expended on enormous stained glass windows which were being made in Murano. The building was indeed ravenous, swallowing down fortunes, drinking molten gold and dining off beefsteaks of silver.

Carried away by a kind of infatuation, the Society seemed to have lost its bearings, and poured money into the Meeting Place without thought or discretion and went about emptying its coffers at a dizzying speed. The gun business was bought by a Russian multinational, the homeopathic product line by an entrepreneur from California. Funds were funnelled in from right and left, vaults once full were swept clean, so not even a coin remained.

When Nesler reported to the architect that the Society had divested its portfolios of most of its holdings, the latter merely shrugged his shoulders. Due to his ambitions, the unannounced grandeur of the structure, more money would need to be found. Construction was expensive, and it was vital that the flow of cash continue unabated.

And that accountant, that individual with eyeglasses and yellow skin whose clothes never seemed to fit, felt himself equal to the task.

Nesler was swept away by his own enthusiasm. He had been the most resistant to the architect, but once converted, that black belt in financial jujitsu would have spilled the blood of his entrails for the man. He had become the most avid henchman, ready to go to almost any lengths for the cause, restlessly searching for funds—willing to dive to the bottom of the sea for a few coins and traverse deserts to lay hands on a soiled banknote or two. In almost constant motion, he went from place to place, travelling over the face of the earth at great speed. He scraped together rupees in India and filled his hat full of kronor in Sweden, shaking hands with others like an automaton, rattling off little speeches and then climbing into a taxi to make his way to the next destination—whether it were some great institution where he hoped to gain millions—or the house of some destitute widow that he might pillage of its silverware.

He would beg five-franc pieces, convince welfare mothers to crack open the piggy banks of their youngsters, and elderly couples to donate their pensions. In Third World countries he stepped through lanes that abounded in itchy dogs, squeezed the last bits of copper out of peasants' purses, emptied the begging bowls of lepers and then, come evening, could be seen at some dinner of important people, whispering into the ears of old women and pestering prominent men as they made their way to the toilet.

He stayed in cut-price hotels, dined at street stands, filling his belly with the meanest viands so as to have a few more pennies to bring back to Switzerland—squeezing his thin lips around fly-blown pakora and inflating his paunch with lentils and other pulses—anything that would provide his frame with energy on the cheap.

Bill by bill, coin by coin he gathered up funds, passing the cap at Körnosophical societies around Europe, browbeating members, frightening them with threats of cosmic retribution and promising lands of jewelled fruits as recompense for compliance. Like a good salesman, he would tell a person anything, as long as he left with their money—seething at the mouth like a rabid dog, howling like a jackal, the pockets of his over-sized trousers bulging with wadded-up bank notes and greasy centimes.

He caught planes and took rail transport, scurrying about, briefcase in hand, the eternal cheap grey suit hanging about his person, the same phrases upon his lips at every doorstep.

"We are asking you to dig deep in order to help defray expenses incurred by the construction of the Meeting Place. Your gift will be used to bring light into a dark world. I am sure you realise how costly equipment is, how quality materials need to be paid for and how numerous the expenses are in such a grand scheme, and if you could manage to give us just thirty or forty percent of the capital you have on hand, it would be helpful."

One day he arrived by bicycle rickshaw at the home of a registered member in Khajuraho, India—a small, two-room dwelling in the middle of a great field—in the distance temples dedicated to Brahma and Vishnu—buildings that looked like elaborate cake decorations, as if they were made of icing, of buttercream and sugar.

He was greeted by the owner, one Tushar Biswas, with exaggerated politeness and offered tea.

"Let me introduce you to my family," the man said. "This is my wife, and these are my three children. This gentleman here is my brother-in-law, Ashok, who lives here together with my sister and their children—which number two."

Nesler looked over the ensemble gathered before him, who all bowed deeply, except for the small children, who gazed up at him in wonder.

"So, nine of you live here together?"

"Indeed we do. It is very fortunate that my job pays me twenty-thousand rupees a year, for regrettably Ashok is out of work, and I am the one privileged to support us all."

"Yes, that is along the lines of what I have come here to talk to you about."

"Proceed," the Indian said, becoming suddenly quite serious.

"You are aware that we are building, in Switzerland, a great meeting place for the members?"

"I most certainly am, and I was delighted to have been able to make a small donation of one-thousand rupees towards defraying the expenses."

"For which we are all of course very grateful. Unfortunately, the sum will not suffice. We are asking for further funds."

"Further funds?"

"Naturally. Whatever you have laid away."

"Only a very small amount—a few thousand rupees which I have put aside for my daughter's dowry," he said, casting his glance at a thin girl of about twelve who stood shyly off to the side with her hands behind her back.

"Fine. That will do to start, and you can donate more when you receive your next wages."

He then climbed back into his rickshaw and went away, the family gazing after him as his driver pedalled on with all of his force, the vehicle bouncing over ruts and then climbing over a rise. The Swiss gentleman still had six more visits to make in the area before dark.

XXII.

It was fall. The forests below displayed their yellow and bronze leaves and smoke began to rise up from distant chimneys while the sun hung somewhat low in the sky—slowly, clumsily making its way from one side of the horizon to the other.

Peter, holding a stack of notebooks under one arm, visited Nachtman in his tent. The latter was lazily smoking a cigarette, gazing dreamily into space while a dying fly buzzed about the room.

"I have come to mention something to you," the young man said.

"Mention away."

"Have you ever considered flying buttresses?"

The question seemed to awaken the architect from his abstraction. He looked significantly at the other.

"Are you in a humorous mood this morning?"

"No. Well, you see . . . I have been doing some calculations. . . ."

"Your first mistake."

". . . And the changes you have written into your plan—the extra towers and expansion of the dome—will add a significant amount of unexpected weight, especially the great cap stone. The walls might not be able to support this. Flying buttresses would——"

"Be both unnecessary and look absurd," Nachtman interrupted. "It seems to me young man, that you have presumed a great deal too much! You are my assistant, not my advisor."

"I only thought . . ."

"Your second mistake. It is an unpleasant habit which you must learn to repress if you wish to continue working for me. Use your ears and mouth in their proper ratio and you will learn a great deal. But do not advise me. This project is visionary, and I will not move a damned aesthetic centimetre from the path I have set!"

Peter bowed his head and, murmuring an apology, made his way from the tent.

He walked forward, towards that eccentric mass of walls and scaffolding, that confusion of men and machines which struggled against stone, seemed to be battling with earth and sky in order to achieve something impossible, to fulfil some kind of egotistical dream of which even they were not aware.

He looked at all this and felt utterly lost—like one without home or family—like a man with sight living in the Valley of the Blind. He had read Körn and felt stimulated by the man's intellectualism. But what he saw around him was anything but intellectual. These were people who felt rather than reasoned, who were chained to each other by emotions—by hidden fears and the strange quivering of their subverted egos. He often wished that he too could be so, with faith in the impossible. For astral bodies and pantheons of winged deities did seem to him just that, and when he asked himself truly about the existence of God, about the possibility of the soul voyaging on after death, he had to admit that he was a non-believer. And, though he did not despise those who thought differently, he could not manage to fully align himself with those who believed it all without either reason or pragmatic proof.

But this he could forgive if the building, the great structure, were completed—for in the end his religion, his cult, was that of stone and steel, of towers and high-rises, sandblasted aluminium and high-gloss steel.

There were however certain things that bothered him. He had done his math and could not help but think that the grand dome that was soon to rise out of the structure proper was being put up on slightly unsound principles. He recalled the words of Fabrizi, about buildings requiring not faith, but science, and found himself suffering from that most terrible of things: doubt.

"Trudy would probably not approve of me," he thought.

And he very well might have been correct.

XXIII.

- Nachtman scurried about in a constant state of excitement, intoxication, sometimes staggering around the structure with a whip in hand, at others wielding a giant bull-horn, into which he would exhale oaths mixed with technical lingo, a vocabulary riveted with screws and armed with hammers. Drunk on both spirits and power, he seemed to have dismissed the fact that he was a mere mortal and stood before the world a deformed Titan—a man-eater endowed with proto-cosmic knowledge.
- He spent his evenings drinking heavily and listening to Swiss-German music—frenzied folk tunes bespeaking the glories of fresh air—spirited marches, waltzes and yodels;—the sound of the Schwyzerörgeli, the jolly Swiss accordion, seemed ever present, frenetic and bizarre as it accompanied him on these bouts of drinking wherein his head became some monumental dome and his eyes scraped against the sky.
- Maria curled herself up at his feet, great misshapen lumps clogged with hair. She had dark circles around her eyes, and her face, having become very pale and thin, made it seem as if Nachtman had inserted his bayonet-like

proboscis into her and sucked the very blood from her veins—this woman who had foolishly laid herself down in his nest, thrown open her arms and wildly exposed her breasts to that feeder.

- The building itself seemed to tremble, sigh—quiver like an embryo, stretch out its wings like a bat. Sometimes, deep in the blackness of night, Nachtman could be seen wandering around its premises, placing himself in its midst, eructing yeasty fumes. He spoke to it, dribbled coddling words onto its walls and invested its heights with strange romantic phrases that seemed to have been leeched from the poetry of Dante.

XXIV.

Peter did not question Nachtman's genius, but he had begun to seriously question the administration of the project. Fortunes were being swallowed up by the building. He knew that many people had given money that they could ill-afford to part with. And then he also realised that, though the work had progressed at an astounding pace, there was still a good deal to be done and the future seemed uncertain. The workers were overworked. Herr Nachtman drove them like slaves. His ambitions seemed to outstretch the imagination, launching themselves into the vague wilderness of what seemed like impossibility.

The thing that oppressed young de la Tour the most was not the fact that the architect was cruel. Though he himself was a gentle enough soul, he was not completely adverse to the idea of human sacrifice. He considered art to be more valuable than compassion. When it came to ethical questions, he was monochrome. Moral considerations were easily pushed aside by those cerebral.

No, it was not Nachtman's indifference to human suffering that bothered him most, but rather something else.

Architecture is a science, and has its laws. They are mathematical and precise. There are truths that are always true.

The young man was, as has been pointed out, fascinated by Nachtman's scheme. He had no doubt that this was a great and noble undertaking. But he saw, as has been noted, certain inconsistencies in his master's calculations. He had tried, very humbly, to point these out, but the architect had not been willing to take into account the logic of his conclusions, seeing in them the ambitious meddling of an inferior.

Peter's temperament was not one of unquestioning loyalty, even less was he a man of undying faith. His mind, exceedingly active, was too keen to let itself be blinded by matters extra-intellectual. And he was stubborn and felt it his duty to make sure the building would be finished with success and maybe there was even some pride at play at having discovered flaws in the plans of his master.

Nachtman was on the south side of the structure, standing with legs wide apart and gazing up towards the heights before him.

Peter approached.

"Mr. Nachtman," he said.

The other did not reply, but seemed lost in meditation.

"Herr Nachtman," was repeated.

"Yes, I am here," the architect said moodily, turning a sharp gaze towards the young man.

"It will soon be time to begin on the dome."

"Indeed it will. We are about to cross the Rubicon."

"I know that you asked me not to mention this again, but . . ."

"If you have something to say, then spit it out."

"My calculations regarding stress . . ."

The architect looked at him blankly.

"My calculations regarding stress," the young man repeated. "I have crunched the numbers in many different ways, and have come to the conclusion that, if we build the dome as planned, its weight could be too great for——"

"*Basta!*"

"For——"

"Listen you jealous little idiot," Nachtman said, decapitating the other's phrase, "you are here to assist me, and yet it seems that you wish to hinder me, to steal my glory with your feminine trembling, with the cowardly ways you learned from those sciolists which at the schools they refer to as professors. I need an eagle by my side, and you are a butterfly. I had hoped to find in you a lion, but instead I see that you are a grub,"

"But if my conscience tells me——"

"Your conscience, you young bastard! You want to speak of your conscience? I'll beat it out of you!"

And so saying, he began striking the young man, slapping his cheeks and rapping his head, kicking him in the shins and stomping on his toes.

"Herr Nachtman!" Peter cried out.

"Get out of here," the other cried out viciously. "You are unwanted! Get off my building site. I don't want to see you here anymore. You make me want to vomit."

Peter was about to say another word in his defence, but looking over noticed several of the Company of Good Men, who had apparently been alerted by Nachtman's raised voice, coming to lend their assistance.

And so the young man retreated, his feelings genuinely hurt.

XXV.

The doors were brought under discussion, Nachtman revealing sketches of two enormous panels vaguely resembling those in the old Kong film—things indeed that looked as if they would be made to keep in check some gargantuan monster rather than serve to adorn a gateway of learning and human understanding.

"Magnificent!" Enheim said with enthusiasm.

"Yes," Maria agreed, "the entrance is, in a sense, the most important part of the structure, and no trouble should be spared to make it extraordinary."

"Are they to be done in bronze?" Borromeo asked.

Nachtman smiled enigmatically before proceeding:

"These doors should be made of something really special—wrought from a sturdy yet precious substance—not gold or platinum or anything of that nature—but a decidedly masculine metal. Something that will geo-magnetically orient the whole, tapping into the earth's currents and attracting men as a flower does bees."

"What do you propose?"

"Iron."

"A sturdy material, yes, but hardly precious."

"Certainly it is said that this element, this ferrum as the ancient Roman's called it, is the sixth most abundant in the universe. But I am not speaking of ordinary iron, but rather of the bones of the gods, a variety more precious than platinum—a variety of iron mined not from the bowels of the earth, but from individuals, from mortal shafts."

"Human mines?"

"Precisely. The average human has around five grams of iron in their body. This is approximately how much iron it takes to make a single nail."

"You wish to make nails?"

"No. The door, my friends, should be distilled from the blood of disciples—those disciples deemed most worthy."

There was a significant moment of silence.

"It is an original idea," Dr. Enheim said, running his hand through his lush beard.

"On principle I am not opposed to it," Borromeo added, "but there are obviously many technical complications."

"Leave that to me."

"We could take out a subscription," Nesler added eagerly. "They could donate their blood while, at the same time, making over their earthly possessions to the Society."

"Yes, we could call it the Ten-Thousand Club, or something of that sort."

And as it was said, so it was done—with old men from Russia being drained of their living fluid, so they could live again, cast in those two huge panels, where their iron would merge with that of rich widows from Australia and forlorn millionaires whose home was the Midwest United States. The fluid arrived in large oil drums and was distilled, using a high gradient magnetic separator, in a laboratory in Zürich—the metal then being transported to Milan where Nachtman personally saw to its smelting.

The members of the board themselves, in order to show solidarity, each donated a pint of blood, and waited eagerly for the material to come back from the chemist. When it did, there was but a small amount of iron dust, greyish and slightly lustrous, resting in a glass vile.

"It is so little," Borromeo commented.

"Yes, there is not much of it," Nesler agreed, holding the glass tube up to the light and examining it.

"That may be," said Dr. Enheim, with a strange glow in his eyes, "but in a hundred thousand years, when our spirits will have long before made their home in the highest spheres of paradise, this bit of iron might be all that remains of us here on earth and will be part of the doors which usher aspirants into the realm of knowledge."

The iron, once smelted, was cast into panels and wrought into ornate bars. And the doors revealed themselves: huge monstrosities, each embossed with a knocker such as a Titan might use—giant rings which themselves were half the height of a man. The hinges were each about a meter high, and the panels were decorated with cast scenes of bulls fighting, women dancing, men tossing spears, while the mullions were in the form of great serpents which twined themselves around bizarre trees which, bare of branch, were shocks of sharp, geometrical patterns, clusters of knotted thunderbolts.

XXVI.

It was early evening in late November when Peter called on Trudy, rang the bell of Enheim's lakeside villa in Lugano. She came to the door, but did not invite him in.

"I cannot speak to you," she said.

"But why not?"

"I do not think it would be approved of."

"So you too hate me!"

"I cannot like you if you are disapproved of by the Society as a whole. My life is, after all, not my own."

"That's not true."

"It is. And for you, your only hope is to throw yourself at the feet of the architect, the good Herr Nachtman, and beg forgiveness. Otherwise you are lost."

"But I did nothing wrong, so how can I ask forgiveness?"

"You are not willing to examine yourself—to look at your soul. You are too proud. You do not have faith in those with more knowledge than yourself and, without faith, deliverance from materiality and ignorance is impossible."

"I won't ask for forgiveness."

She pressed her lips tightly together.

"Trudy . . ."

"Goodbye Peter," she said hurriedly, and shut the door.

Peter turned and walked away, turned towards the city centre, hands in pockets, legs leading him forward, more by their own volition than his. He walked along the Viale Castagnola, past the Società Navigazione, and then on, past the park, leafless trees looking stark and hundred-year-old pines, cone-shaped, thrusting themselves high up and sniffing at the fading light of dusk.

He then entered the city centre, walked by a giant block of marble, a grid of large plate glass windows lit in neon, totally incongruous amidst the surrounding eighteenth-century buildings. In the daytime one could look in and see the office workers at work—an unfortunate trend in European architecture: the office worker as caged animal.

Elegant looking women tripped along in high heels. Grave-looking men with gelled hair and black overcoats marched forward, smoking cigarettes, letting their loud voices be sucked up by mobile phones to be transmitted across land and sea. Every being was full of their own importance and strode over the earth like gods—a mass of delusion, blindness, the intoxication of streets and essentially boxlike constructions with roofs and windows, the madness of men as they surge together, like braids of worms agitated with life, thrilled by their own quivering muscles and their ability to make gurgling noises.

The bars were full of people having aperitivos: leaning against counters, sipping white wine, Campari and soda, drinking beer out of thin, cone-shaped glasses, munching on

[1] *kkkkkkkkkkkkkkkkkkkkkkkkkkkkkkkkkkkkkkkkkkkkkkkkkkkkkkk*

finger-sandwiches and doing their ritualistic mating dance, of which lubricating their digestive tracts, grinning like clowns, was of primary importance.

For some reason, all this life filled Peter with ineffable sadness—as if he were watching condemned men eat their last meals before their veins were pumped full of poison. The faces seemed like so many masks which hid desiccated skulls and the laughter seemed like the futile squeak of door hinges.

He hurried on, walked along Via Nassa, through the arcades, and recalled how this area had once been where fishermen lived. Now it was a long array of jewellery shops and expensive boutiques. Silver, gold and diamonds sparkled in the windows. Fibreglass mannequins found themselves bound in expensive and rather ugly clothing. Apricot foulards and blue polyvinyl chloride pants which would cling to the skin.

In one particularly elegant shop, a watch designed by a prominent Swiss architect was on display—a giant hunk of silver, grotesque—and an extravagant price tag hung limply to one side, seeming pale and debauched.

He gazed on this piece of equivocal jewellery and thought of Nachtman's words. Indeed, the art of architecture had been in a large way debased. The man had been right about that. But for all the high-minded talk he had spewed forth, it seemed to Peter that that strange man himself, with his ample belly and ape-like arms, was lampooning the great art, turning it into a nauseous joke of more than elephantine proportion.

When the god is taken from its pedestal, there is nowhere to put it but in the latrine. If Peter would not worship Nachtman, he would despise him. There was no place for an in-between.

It was now dark. The light had completely abandoned the day.

Finally he arrived at the chiesa. The building, probably the oldest in that area of town, was a true breath of fresh air. Its simple lines calmed him. Yes, he thought to himself, this was architecture. Simplicity, without need of pretence. It was a strange object, sitting amidst that nest of banks and jewellery shops along the lake—pushed against by a giant hotel to one side.

The front, with its large oak door and two round windows, reminded him vaguely of a Zuni ceremonial mask, seemed to be connected to some remote and much more sympathetic past.

To the side of the church there was a long series of steps, which led up the side of the hill, flanked by an abandoned tram-line.

"I must talk to Aunt Maria," he told himself.

The steps seemed endless. He was hardly in good shape and half-way up stopped and turned, panting for breath, could feel his underarms and shallow chest exuding moisture.

His eyes wandered instinctively over to that mountain. He could make out the lights burning up there—for a portion of the work continued, even at night. He lowered his gaze, let it rest on the lake where the lights of the city were reflected on the surface of the water. A veritable rainbow of greens, yellows and whites glistening on that vast black sheet.

He turned, climbed the rest of the way up the steps, walked on and was soon ringing his aunt's doorbell.

She answered, was dressed in a flowing gown of blue cotton. Ghostlike, with nothing but a hesitant whisper on her lips, she let him enter.

The place was illumined solely with candles, the wax of which let off an unpleasant aroma, the light of which cast bizarre shadows.

Maria had redecorated the place. Now bad paintings of eyes and pyramids hung from the walls and pseudo-Egyptian statuettes cluttered the mantelpiece and lurched up from the coffee table. Prominent in the living room was a large photo of Körn—one taken about 1920, which showed him with wild eyes, a bowler hat and the beard of a pharaoh. Next to it, a picture of almost equal size of Nachtman was exposed—a pyriform nose which stood before a muddy complexion; a head negligently dressed in wispy white hair.

Without warmth, she offered her nephew a seat.

"It has been some time since you have paid me a visit," she said dully.

"And you wish I had?"

"I did not say that. I was only stating a historical fact."

"So, you have no regrets?"

"I regret that you were so unkind. Not to me. I don't care about that. But to Herr Nachtman, who always treated you in such a fatherly way."

Peter smiled somewhat bitterly, and then, after sweeping his hair back and sitting thoughtful for a moment:

"Aunt Maria, I need to talk to you."

"I thought that is what you were doing."

"I fear that the Society is going too far . . . trusting this man too much."

"But you yourself said that you thought he was the greatest architect that ever lived!"

"And so he is. But he is also . . . insane."

"Peter, he is the man I love. He is a sorcerer! He is as profound as Jesus, as wise as Parshvanatha!"

"I think he is dangerous."

"Which makes him all the more exciting. You are only bitter because he has, quite rightly, expelled you from the works. And now you come here . . ."

"Aunt, you should break with him."

"Never. He is the only *real* man I have ever known. You are only a child and are still ignorant . . . of the functioning of a woman's heart. And are surely jealous. Because he is a genius, and you . . ."

Peter bit his bottom lip. And then said: "So be it. If you want to destroy yourself, then I cannot stop you."

Maria stood up very erect. She had obviously been stung by his words.

"Destroy myself?" she hissed. "Do you know what stupid things you are saying? Who are you to lecture anyone? It was you who first introduced me to Herr Nachtman. It was you who first brought him to the Society. . . . You were always so forward-thinking, open-minded. And now listen to you. You talk like an old man. Though you are young, you are completely without spirit—an insect and a coward who does not believe in God! Yes, get out of here, go and bury yourself in the earth—and don't come to me anymore."

XXVII

The scene was something that could have only been painted by a Breughel or a Bosch. The scale of the structure dwarfed the workers, made them appear less significant than insects—ants or skipping fleas. Dozens of comedio-tragedies were being played out at every moment. A man let out a violent scream, his leg crushed to pudding by a large block of granite. Men scaled ladders, sat perched atop half-built walls, held hammers, hoisted loads. Olaf Lidskog, the old Swedish millionaire, could be seen high up on the walls, his beard being swept about by the wind. With his thin frame and wild eyes, he seemed like some holy man—some ascetic undergoing a bizarre penance as a few flakes of snow drifted down from the sky.

It was so much trouble for the workers to get to the top that, once there, they had to stay for as long as possible, eating their lunch and dinner and often even sleeping in small hammocks in that precarious position, suspended hundreds of meters in the air. Of course falls were not in the least bit unusual, occurring on an almost daily basis. Mutilated corpses had to be scraped from the earth with such regularity that there was even a special work unit set with the task and those who perished in such a manner were referred to as martyrs and it was said that their souls graduated instantly to the twelfth plane where an extraordinary place was reserved for them and they were given audience with certain advanced spirits.

Once prominent businessmen were reduced to unshaven, dirty, half-naked specimens. Beautiful women saw their breasts dry up. Men were broken, women crushed. And yet, thanks in part to those disciplinary measures previously mentioned, not a complaint was now heard. These disciples of the great philosophy accepted the hardship with joy, convinced that their beings were being cleansed, that they were mounting, together with the structure itself, ever higher into the realms of spiritualism.

The building itself seemed no longer a place to worship God, but seemed a god itself, around the heights of which the tails of clouds wrapped themselves.

Some said at night they saw it moving, writhing like a snake, puffing like an angry bull. Others said that they had seen angels with long forked tails flying about the incomplete dome and the thing seemed to look over the land with a mighty eye.

It seemed certain that it was possessed, endowed with malicious genius—an insatiate hunger. Its belly seemed to rumble and claws to reach out and grab those around; it would bite off their heads and gorge itself on their blood. Its walls seemed alive, the entrance a huge hungry mouth and at night, when lights were lit inside so work therein could continue, the windows indeed were like so many eyes—an enormous owl with countless heads.

XXVIII.

Nachtman became a sort of cult figure. The project was no longer simply the construction of a building, but rather the construction of a portal which would lead to other spheres—to ethereal lands where vulgar thoughts went not and people lived in flowers, drank the nectar of stars and spent their time performing ecstatic rituals of the spirit.

Claiming that he had been promoted by the astral body of Körn which had visited him in the night, along with other cosmic authorities, the architect declared himself an Ipsissimus, a grand master, and indeed no one dared contradict him. On the contrary, Enheim, the great spiritual scientist himself, after consulting the stream of cosmic consciousness of the Goddess of the City of Erech and meditating on various luminous particles, gave him a ritual coronation which consisted of mulberries and oil of hyssop being smeared over his chest while the four-thousand ritual syllables were chanted. And, finally, a helmet crowned with peacock feathers was placed on his head.

"I, Commander Adeptus Magus, the Lightbearer," Enheim pronounced gravely, the words flowing from the depths of his beard like commandments from on high, "who am in possession of the knowledge of the most remote times, have received messages from the Blue Star, giving me full and unabated permission for today's coronation. Henceforth, your spiritual name will be Brother XII and you will be known as an agent of the Supreme Self.

The architect smiled broadly and hugged all around him, pressing them to his great belly with an admirable semblance of love. That night he drank heavily of brandy and in the days that followed regurgitated every mystical utterance he had ever heard, let out a stream of plagiarisms[1] gleaned from a remarkably wide variety of religious texts—passages gutted of all meaning which he laced together and hung all around him—garlands of hypocrisy that sweated elixated fruits and which he admixed with architectural terms, building palaces of grand phrases which left his audience in awe—believing this rubbish to be gold, believing this charlatan to be the one true messenger as he spoke of metaphysical bungalows and pneumatic turrets, of extramundane high-rises where the soul might ascend and supersensible dungeons done in whiplash curves where the disobedient would plunge to be skewered and roasted on spits.

Through a sort of mass hypnotism, all obeyed him who was referred to as Brother XII blindly. He had a private cook, a man from Bavaria, who was able to work miracles with a saucepan and prepared him liver of burbot and omelets of ambergris, partridges stuffed with frankincense and batter-fried eel larvae. Designated colony females, married or single, were to mate with Brother XII up to nine times, and roll with him on beds of verbena—an activity which Maria herself fully approved of, convinced as she was of the architect's saintly qualities. And indeed his spectacular vices had something grand

[1] . . . beyond the scourges over my thoughts which are like planed columns, clinging to knowledge of the truth . . .

about them—something truly supramundane which recalled those ancient Roman emperors who claimed themselves to be descendants of gods and spat upon morality and temperance alike as with drunken laughter they set men aflame, dined off the naked backs of prostitutes and demanded obedience from both moon and sun, shoving stars into the facial orifices of their lovers while reciting long and dreary poems that put their page boys to sleep.

Sometimes he would stroll about in a long white gown humming the refrain from Übere Gotthard flüget Bräme. He drank expensive whisky by the gallon and ate the genital glands of sea anemones stewed in white wine. He seemed to relish his role as mystic and, claiming himself to be the embodiment of transcendent reality, declared that he was the Knight of the Red Eagle, Grand Inquisitor Commander, who would lead people to fabulous lands.

"Listen to me, my friends," he said to the disciples. "I am your guardian angel and will guide you straight up there to the sky, to the ethereal dimensions. We are building something more than just a shield from rain and sun. We are building a ladder on which to climb to the stars. This is the tabernacle—you have arrived!"

Maria kissed his every part, and Nachtman, thinking to make her a worthy queen, fashioned her Madame Why, Inspectress of Rights and Degrees, and she would go about in a dress dripping with fringe, followed by an elite group of her Sisters of Future Well-being, who attended to her every want. She fumigated the building site regularly with lichen and cassia bark and dispensed oils of cardamom and evening primrose in abundance.

Enheim, propelled forward on this tide of the occult, braided his beard and wore a burnoose and walked about with a rope around his waist like a Capuchin monk, lending his voice to the adherents, offering words of encouragement to those sons and daughters of men as they struggled against hunger and huddled at night around fires of twigs.

He and the architect threw off all modesty, proclaiming themselves geniuses, emissaries of both space and time. Enheim, in the end, had gladly let himself be cast in a slightly subordinate position, for even there the heights he stood at were dizzying, the rarefied atmosphere of power intoxicating.

Nachtman mounted the podium of supremacy with the naturalness of a king, usurping the individuality of those around him with a kind of stolid glee, a greediness as profound as the universe itself—vast and seemingly endless.

Enheim, concerned about the well-being of his daughter, put forward the possibility of a marriage agreement with the architect.

"But a man likes to maintain his freedom," the latter said.

"Yes, but you are no longer young. It is time that you thought of settling down."

"She likes older men, does she?"

"She needs a man who is spiritually developed."

"Well, I'll think about it," Nachtman said, caressing the tip of his bulbous nose with one finger.

XXIX.

It was August and the heat extreme. The sun shone, hot, violent—shooting its rays to the earth like arrows. The mountain seemed as if it had been shoved in some great inferno and enveloped in flames. Several of the workers had died of heat stroke. Tongues hung from open mouths and naked torsos glistened with sweat.

Due to the fact that there were so many perspiring men, an unpleasant odour filled the air, like that of rotten fruit. Flies buzzed lazily about, sometimes falling exhausted to the earth where their wings and labella agitated disagreeably. Birds were just about cooked in their nests and moles and other burrowing creatures dug themselves deep underground.

Nachtman sat in front of his tent, listening to the sounds of Res Schmid and sipping at a heavily iced gin and tonic which was crowned with a sprig of mint. A woman kneeled before him, massaging his naked feet.

Nesler appeared. The hems of his trousers were covered with dust. A tie hung limp around his bloated neck and his face looked as if it had been rubbed with oil. He seemed like a man who had traversed a desert—walked over dunes and suffered in storms of sand.

"I need to talk to you," he said in an agitated voice.

The architect waved the young woman away, slipped his feet into a pair of clogs and led the other into his tent, where three or four fans were whirring away, creating a pleasant breeze.

"A drink?"

"A glass of water if you have one," the other said, wiping sweat off his forehead with a dull-coloured handkerchief.

Nachtman poured the other a glass of water and refreshed his own drink.

"So what seems to be bothering you, my friend?"

"I have tried . . ."

"Tried?"

"I have tried, tried so very hard to pull together the money for the completion of the project. And many millions have I brought to you."

"You have done very well."

"But I am at the end of my resources. The structure has devoured the savings of just about every member on earth." Nesler waved his arms around in the depths of his sleeves. "But now our coffers are empty. We have no money—not even enough to buy the stone needed to finish this building!"

Nachtman was silent. The blades of the fans spun. He tapped his fingernails on his desk and looked thoughtful—his eyes narrowing, the gear teeth of his mind biting one against the next.

"Then other materials will have to be found," he said presently.

"Other materials?"

"Yes. Something for which we will not need to pay and which, far from diminishing this great structure, will add to its glory."

"But I cannot think of . . ."

"There is dirt, wet earth, out of which adobe could be made."

"Not a very noble substance."

"And one we shall not use, for there is another, just about as common, that appeals to my artistic sensibilities much more—one which I have dreamed of using since my youth when I was despised for being a genius." His eyes gleamed like the blade of an axe. "Endowed with an extra-keen sense of vision, I have seen humans as they really are. Our ancestors built their dwellings out of mud and brush. Inuits use ice to make their igloos; African tribesman grasses to make their huts. Resources are always at hand—if one will just look for them. The temple of Huaca del Sol was made entirely of dirt and straw. Tiles. Bricks. Thoughtless entities whose only material fault is being suffused with water like sponges. As I see it, we have over 100,000 dedicated followers. If all their bones were piled up, if their flesh was desiccated and cubed . . ."

"You mean to say . . ."

"Yes! We shall complete the structure, complete the dome with human flesh, with skeletal tissue, give this creature I have dragged from my mental womb the blood it needs to wet its veins and expand its lungs."

XXX.

There were many volunteers, many who wished to entomb themselves in this monument—to immortalize themselves in that great building. Brick plants were set up in Sri Lanka and South Africa, in South America and Australia, and thereby, for a very low cost, the bricks were transported by a Chinese shipping company aboard five-story 4,250-ton cargo boats to the ports of Genova and Trieste from where they were trucked to the building site.

In Columbia, after attending an all-night candlelight meditation, the applicants convened at the factory. Presently they were moved through a gate, moulded into a single-file line. One by one, after joyfully hugging each other, convinced they would be meeting each other shortly in a plane of great refinement where there was nothing but spirit, without materiality to hinder either love or progress, they entered into an aluminium structure where they were required to take up a captive bolt pistol and self-apply it to their foreheads. They were told to visualise a cross between their eyes and apply the barrel of the pistol there. Upon pressing the trigger, a pointed bolt was propelled forward at a velocity of 75 m/s by the power of pressurised air, penetrating the forehead and destroying the cerebrum and part of the cerebellum. They were then fed into a large machine which reduced them to a pulp, a mixture with the appearance and texture of oatmeal. After being mixed with straw they were placed in molds and set out to dry in the tropical sun.

Back in Switzerland, a new momentum was added to the work—it seemed that it had taken on a new significance. Never had the feeling of brotherhood been stronger. It seemed indeed that humanity was finally progressing, finally ridding itself of its egoism, and men were at last learning to give themselves for the common good.

Up there on that high mountain, the people worked, placing the bodies of their comrades on that noble structure, mumbling prayers and humming lugubrious melodies, intoxicated by the scheme they were taking part in. Those strange pieces of adobe that represented countless dreams—the hopes of mothers, the pride of fathers—whole populations reduced to oblong cubes—those bizarre objects in which, upon close inspection, fingers and toes and strands of hair could be seen, were stacked one atop the other, wedged together, and in this process one could almost see the crowding together, nose pressed against nose, cheek crushed against cheek, beings mashed together in claustrophobic tightness, no space even for their tears, no room for them to so much as gasp.

XXXI.

The third winter was a mild one, without snow, frighteningly warm.

In late February lightning ripped the sky and down came the rain, forming sheets of water which dashed themselves against the structure and the wind gave shrill cries while earth was swept away and tents collapsed.

The workers trudged through mud, water running down their faces. People slipped. One man broke his arm and lay there in the brown muck screaming. Groups of humans clustered together, shivering, their hair plastered against their skulls.

And then, after some days, the storm exhausted itself, the clouds and mist disappeared.

Around the building all was sludge. All the trees had been chopped down. The place looked like a battlefield. The humans were filthy, cold, their clothing reduced to rags. They spoke almost exclusively in grunts and monosyllables and loped along rather than walked, occasionally electrified by the commanding voice of Nachtman, who looked on them more like stones with legs than creatures of bones and meat. Tears rolled down their faces and they smiled like idiots—fools who could not differentiate misery from joy.

They piled up those bricks of their brothers and sisters from foreign parts, but soon those worthy beings abroad willing to sacrifice themselves were exhausted, old and young alike, from the tip of Tierra del Fuego to the heights of Greenland, from the grasslands of Mongolia to the Cape of Good Hope. Whole families had given themselves and, in one case, an entire village in Bangladesh, and shipload upon shipload of bricks had been transported to the mountain and hoisted up—to block out the sun and sky, obscure the stars at night and shield the world below from moonbeams.

"It seems our supply of bricks has almost come to an end," Nesler said to the architect.

"Well, the work is not far from finished. We only need another forty or fifty thousand."

"But where are we to get them? I have been canvassing all over, and I swear that——"

"But just look around you."

Nesler's eyes shifted from right to left, and then turned themselves upward, taking in a scene of men and women by the thousands, lurking along the base of the walls, crowding the scaffolding, toiling high, high up on the dome and towers which were not far from done.

"The workers . . . ?"

"Precisely. We will simply bring their functionality to the ultimate conclusion."

And so it came to pass that the workers themselves were called on and, starved, brainwashed, desperate, were more than glad to sacrifice themselves, to throw themselves bodily into that rising volcano, the Meeting Place. Tales were told of the great dimensions they would visit once their souls had been purified, had been converted into a highly ethereal substance which could travel at light years a second—visit alien races—frolic through the skies like comets. Enheim lectured them on the beauties of the higher dimensions, where cities were built atop huge lotuses which rested on crystal lakes and gentle clouds of nectar encircled the spires of luxurious edifices where the inhabitants might relax, distending themselves on cushions of sweet-smelling moss while listening to the melodious music of cosmic harps.

"On the twelfth plane which, due to your sacrifices, you will soon visit, there is no sorrow, sickness or pain. You will be endowed with a luminous body which itself will have fourteen senses, including moral receptors, receptors that can communicate with sub-atomic particles, and others that can sense ultraviolet light. There are plants there of exquisite beauty the fruits of which are sweeter than any substance known on earth and contain certain subtle nutrients which your light bodies can feed off of with great joy. You will leave behind a dark ugly world, corrupted by greed and egoism, to enter a place where all live together, bathing in ponds of harmony."

Trudy, who was there, listened to her father with a far-away expression in her eyes. The old Swede pushed himself forward with the utmost eagerness, so as to be first of those present to become an eco-friendly building material that would take almost nothing from the earth and this gentleman was followed by many thousands. Then there were some few others who were less eager, and the weaker of these, those who were almost useless, were herded into open pens and made to do what they would not do by free will. But by and large, the people gave their lives eagerly, pushing against each other so as to be at the forefront of the horrible surrender, eagerly forfeiting the forms their mothers had given them to become cubed—to become blocks that would make up the edifice—mere material without either personality or thought—without the ability to move or breath—without life.

Nachtman's bizarre dreams seemed to have pushed themselves out of his cranium and grown exponentially into this dark and brooding thing that jutted up out of the earth, fed on prayers and derangement and groped at the heavens as if trying to claw out the entrails of the very gods themselves.

XXXII.

"She can serve a period of apprenticeship and then we will see," the architect said.

"But she is a good girl. She would make a wonderful wife. Her desserts are excellent."

"As I said, I am willing to give her a trial."

And so it was that Enheim's daughter washed the feet of the architect, made him sweets, sacrificed her lips and even attempted to give him her heart, but he, who had so many of the opposite sex at his disposal, was anything but entertained—found her insipid and, in the end, determined that a marriage with the young lady would be a dull and unnecessary business.

"I think being a bachelor is my destiny," he said to the doctor.

"But . . ."

"The structure needs to be completed. She would be more useful putting her hands to good use instead of baking me cookies."

The next day Enheim informed his daughter that, at least for the present, she was to remain single.

Trudy took her father by the hand. He leaned over and kissed her forehead, caressing her young face with his thick beard. Together they gazed at the structure before them—at the workers who were in the process of finishing the great dome with the fleshcrete of their recently accepted comrades—at the works near at hand, where others were queued up to be processed, transformed into building material.

"Ah, it will not be long before it is finished," he said.

"I am proud of you, father. You have done so much."

"I have done what I can."

"Father, I wish to be amongst their number."

Enheim looked at his daughter in astonishment.

"I want to give myself to the cause," she continued.

"Absolutely not. I forbid it!"

"But why, when you have spoken of the wonderful things beyond?"

"Because, er, it would be unsuitable."

"I cannot think of anything more suitable than for the daughter of the Commander Adeptus Magus to sacrifice her meaningless body in order to receive a body of light on the twelfth plane."

The doctor threw up his hands in frustration.

"The answer is no," he declared. "And that is completely final. There are enough workers willing to do this without you. Your sacrifice is not needed. Not in any way needed!"

XXXIII.

Other members, those with the oddest figures—the ugly, the ridiculous—the hunchbacks and strange gaunt giants with lantern jaws, were chosen to be the grotesques, chosen to be mounted as gargoyles on the outside walls. These he, the Knight of the Red Eagle, invested, suffocated in latex and plaster and then burned out their bodies at high temperature before immortalizing them in bronze and aluminium—frightful statues that still retained the contortions of death, the grimaces of pain. These were then mounted high up on the outside in the hundreds. There were figures which cringed and figures which threw open their arms wildly, faces distorted, with wide eyes and sickening grins. Some with outstretched hands, others shrinking away; or with mouths open, into which gutters were inserted so that when it rained, the water would spew from their orifices, so that it seemed as if those horrible beings were vomiting endless streams of mucous.

"You see, I also understand beauty," the architect said. "Thus these human beings serve a double purpose. In a utilitarian manner, they give us the material we need to finish the structure. At the same time, they adorn it, giving it a final dazzle that would be difficult not to appreciate. We honour their sacrifice, and entomb them in the building they helped to create, where respects will be paid to their memories for a long time to come."

To add to the wildness, the architect took goats, cows and other farm animals and did the same to them—so a sort of hideous menagerie was formed, where crude bovines sat perched at great heights and chickens, melted together in dozens, appeared like nasty cherubim on the wall arcading.

Then, to further the decoration, many strange beasts were carved in stone: Long worms with human heads; three-headed buffalos; lions with the breasts of women; and gorillas spliced with rams. A chaos of bizarre creatures crept out of the towers and facade, mutations, things that were half insect, half fish, or then again fish with legs and men with fins—an infinite variety of combinations, deformities hatched from nightmares.

XXXIV.

Dr. Enheim burst out of the little train. He rushed forward, following his belly rapidly towards the structure. Borromeo, wearing a pair of shorts and a t-shirt, feet in sturdy leather boots, was there—talking in low tones to one of the few remaining workers, one of the Company of Good Men, one of those mountains of tendons and muscle.

"Where is she? Where is Trudy?" the doctor cried out. "I have been away for a few days. A fundraiser in Zürich. And, upon returning . . ."

Borromeo pointed to a pile of bricks.

"But . . ." Enheim murmured in horror.

"I tried to dissuade her, but she was adamant," the athlete said. "And in the end, who am I to try and block someone's spiritual progress."

"I am speechless."

"I knew you would come, so I set her aside. She is here . . . this one on the left."

The doctor looked at the brick. It was smaller than the others, about 20 × 12 × 6 cm, and in fact did somehow seem to be her, Trudy Enheim, and the doctor, gazing at its surface, thought he could see her soft brown eyes, which were like those of a calf, staring at him from out of its surface, and thought he could hear the thing whispering words and when he took it up, it seemed as if he were touching her small plump hands.

He stood up very straight, his beard before him like a shield. "Now, more than ever," he said, "am I determined to see this project through to the end in a grand style."

"Yes."

"And I personally, with my own hands, will set this brick in place. And high, high up I will put it."

XXXV.

Through self-depravation Maria's luscious body had lost its contours, her cheeks had become concave, her complexion as white as snow. A pale blue tint was seen about her temples and a somewhat darker tone beneath her eyes. Yet this decay added to her beauty, made it profoundly striking, as in the paintings of female martyrs who, with red plasma spurting from open wounds, crowns of thorns and weeds resting on their heads, draw the interest of the opposite sex, who are most attracted to the female in her vulnerable state—a dependent creature that cannot run or hide, who minces forward in high-heels, her thin blood barely warming her meagre muscular tissue, her eyes glazed, languid.

She smiled often, but weakly, pathetically. She had her hair cut short, cropped it like a boy's, so that her long white neck showed. Lost in some sort of pseudo-spiritual cloud, a cloud of incense and self-imposed hallucination, she wandered from the cemetery of her past—where the corpses of her former interests and ambitions lay mouldering—into the dark forest of love, a place in which she shivered under chilly shadows and let her skin be pierced by the eager brambles of that man who would have sooner finished off a wounded fawn than wrestled with a bear; that man who needed flesh, red meat, and was happy that it was there warm on his plate without need to hunt hard for it.

Great loves are disgustingly selfish, and leave room in the heart for none but the adored. The relationship Maria had with Nachtman was one of those bizarre anomalies of nature which would have left Darwin scratching his head.

Kissing the uneven surface of the architect's skull, she would murmur romantic smudges calculated to titillate and then, having collapsed into his arms with an ardour truly frightening, having wrapped her lips around his nose and ears in turn, she would offer herself to him bodily, this woman who had the temperament of a disciple, was as searing as a firebrand. These episodes, as acute as they were alarming, seemed to carry with them something of the cabaret—the disgusting entertainment of Nazi transvestites and leather-clad midgets.

With his gut sticking forward and armpits exhaling effluvia, the architect accepted her love as some deity would a blood sacrifice, gurgling in his intoxication about strange dreams in which he was visited by mahatmas who instructed him on the secrets of the ancient Myceneans and Egyptians and then, wagging a tongue off which cream-coloured spittle slid, he would proceed to sample the morsels of her buffet as outside the sound of work rang on—the gruff cries of the Company of Good Men going up amongst the rattle of hydromechanical work tools.

Then what was love to this man?

It was around half past seven in the morning when she arrived at the work site. She slipped into his tent, went to the bed. A figure was there, beneath the blankets and sheets. She sat down beside it, pressed her hand close. Then it rose up, appeared out of those coverings of cotton and wool—Borromeo, glassy-eyed, muscular chest uncovered.

"Alex isn't here," he said in a sleepy voice. "He's out, looking over the men no doubt."

A moment later, outside the tent, she wiped a tear from her eye.

"I cannot blame him," she murmured to herself. "I cannot expect a genius to be satisfied with my meagre treasures. And if he is happy, I should be. His heart is surely big enough to share and he needs a great many sensations to satisfy his regal appetite."

XXXVI.

Summer had wilted away and now it was, once again, autumn.

The structure itself seemed to be coming to life, gorged as it was with other lives—a huge organic thing with eyes that saw and lungs that breathed. Its shape was hybrid—half animal, half vegetable—something between a gargantuan fungus and an antediluvian lizard. It was such a thing that was impossible to look at without emotion, for it represented all mankind's strongest emotions—was a physical manifestation of fear and hope, of violent passion and sacrifice; a re-enforcement of the awesomeness of the universe—of chaos and the leech-like derangement that is integral to human nature and make this species sweep aside forests, drain oceans, commit nuclear follies, all with the utmost diligence, in the belief that such madness helps it progress.

The board members themselves were feverish, often finding it difficult to speak in full sentences or connect their thoughts. Having channelled so much of their energy, so much of themselves into that building, they had difficulty distinguishing their own selves from the stones and towers.

Maria kissed its very walls and Dr. Enheim, tossing his great belly to the ground, wet its marble floor with his tears.

Nesler, whenever he had a spare moment, went to the temple that was to carry his name, that niche on the east side of the structure, and, gently whistling an air from Schubert, gazed at the place with manifest satisfaction.

As for Borromeo, he strutted from one end of the interior to the other, like a peacock, now sweeping out a corner, now polishing a part of a wall—feeling as one privileged, one who had been touched by the wings of Cassiel and seen the Seventh Heaven, who had been graced by earthquakes and hurricanes, had his strong limbs tempered by the lead and melancholy.

XXXVII.

Another winter had all but passed. A winter even milder than the previous.

Peter walked out of the building, the Academy of Architecture in Mendrisio, with a backpack over one shoulder. While working on the project, he had neglected his studies, in truth even despised his teachers, but now he was back at it, spending his days buried in books, immersed in theory, rather than up on that mountain top where men and machines did battle with earth and sky.

He felt intolerably lonely, had heard what had happened to Trudy, and it saddened him deeply. He tried to imagine that he might at some future time meet her. Might meet her in some other world, where their spirits, golden yellow flames, would flit about, now intertwining, now blending—giving kisses without flesh, making those strange eternal pledges that are the core of religion and love. He tried to imagine, but he could not—could, when it was night, only see in the stars flickers of light from masses of dying plasma, of hydrogen long since extinguished, and in the day, as his feet stepped one before the next, only could he see grim-faced pragmatism that cut the heads off all dreams.

He sniffed and pushed the hair back away from his eyes as he thought about it—continued his way, along the Corso Bello, the facades of the buildings hiding so many old women sunk in apricot-coloured divans mentally caressing their fossilized loves, their memories of springtime; concealing the lean forms of unemployed bachelors whose thoughts roosted in dirty corners; and also concealing stooping lunatics who shambled from side to side. So it is that, shuttered in, lives disappear unseen—buildings being places to hide from the sun and ourselves, private theatres in which we can dramatize—our audience four walls and closed windows.

The street was cobbled. A few bored shopkeepers stood outside their shops. Smoking cigarettes, eyes half-closed, scratching bellies which waited patiently for the dinner hour, when they could be stuffed full of masticated horse flesh, corn mush, cheeses which carried with them the sapidity of marigolds and fresh grass.

Peter felt a hand on his shoulder and turned around.

It was Fabrizio Fabrizi.

He had clearly slid since the young man had last seen him. His cleft chin was unshaven and his blue eyes tinged with red. He wore a pair of dirty jeans and a plaid shirt with the sleeves rolled up so that his forearms were exposed. As he stood before Peter, he swayed slightly, his legs not entirely sure which way the earth was.

"So how is life up there on the mountain?" he asked, a grim note to his voice, a spark of anger in his eyes.

"I don't know. I have left the project—or, rather, been kicked off of it, as I never did put forward a resignation."

"Ah, you too!"

"Yes, I was too voluble with my ideas."

"You were a fool, like me. It's better to keep quiet and let people do what they want. This world wasn't made for men who think. Once you have been fired from such a big project . . . it is difficult to find work again. . . . To draw a pay-cheque. . . . But come and drink a *bianchino* with me."

Peter let himself be led into a nearby bar where the ex-foreman ordered two white wines. The latter clasped one of the small glasses in his large fist and waved it about as he spoke, thrusting forward his chin, deep phrases working themselves out from between his white teeth, from beneath his moustache, which seemed as sharp and aggressive as a cutlass.

"That no one can smell the stench of that pig is beyond me. An ass dredged up from the unemployment roles. But that is how the world works these days. Fools are showered with gold, while honest men are thrown aside. Only superficial, useless things are praised—and that fat criminal, that *zucchino* from the north, is throwing who knows how many millions or billions into that castle of straw that will be blown away at the first strong wind, taking with it all those unskilled monkeys he has clambering all over it."

"So you really think the structure is unsound?"

"Of course it is. But maybe that doesn't even mean a damned thing. The truth is that half the buildings you see around you are only held together by Scotch Tape and miracles. The people who build them make pacts with the devil so the things stay upright until they are led into the world beyond. Buildings are no longer constructed for their usefulness, but simply as an advanced form of capitalism. God willing, one day the people will awake and set fire to the lot of them, burning up the architects, the bosses and buildings all in one go."

With wild eyes he drained off his wine.

XXXVIII.

Nachtman, more than a little tipsy, expelled the woman from his tent—a slim red-head from Ireland, a Sister of Future Well-being. He threw himself down on his bed, closed his eyes, and had a dream.

In this dream he was on a vast, golden plain. Very sharp and colourful plants grew from the arid soil, which was cracked, scarred by fissures. He wandered forward, crossed bizarre gorges in which flowed rivers of cow skulls or dead crows or remnants of giants and soon came to a city, magnificent in every aspect, yet completely abandoned it would seem. In the centre of the city there was a large castle surrounded by a moat. A drawbridge was let down and a gate uplifted. He crossed over and went within the walls, was soon climbing a corkscrew staircase, the sound of his footsteps echoing with instrumental timbre as up and up he went and then it seemed like the steps began to slip beneath his feet, as he agitated his thin legs faster and the music gained tempo.

He was now in the middle of a large room. To the sides were suits of grey armour the helmets of which had large beaks and the hands of which clasped huge halberds with blades shaped like moons and stars. In the centre was a throne and on the throne sat a man. The architect looked closer and recognised the great Dr. Körn.

"I have been watching you," the doctor said.

Nachtman raised his eyebrows. "Well, I have nothing to be ashamed of."

"Your conscience. Through unprejudiced contemplation . . ."

"Let's not use abusive language."

"The Universal Brotherhood of Mankind."

"Do you have something to tell me?"

"Yes. I have a request."

The architect became obsequious. "You know I'll try my best, do whatever I can."

"When you make the altar you must pay attention to certain rhythmic occurrences the ideation of which will result in your casting a statue of me. It should be made of solid bronze and be five cubits in height and four in width. At the base of the statue should be laid a girdle of silk finely woven with pomegranates in scarlet needlework, badger skins dyed red, and pieces of sardius and carbuncle. In the midst of the statue, at the level of the breast, you will put a heart derived from a human entity so that the metabolic process can be fulfilled and the Eastern Star aligned with Venus."

"And then?"

"I am just saying . . . outside the sphere of ordinary consciousness . . ."

A greenish light filled the room as did phosphorescent moths and the architect suddenly felt himself tumbling down stairs, falling through space, clutching at octagonal ghosts and triangular phantoms and the skirts of fast-moving entities which flitted off into the infinite distance.

When he awoke, his temples and underarms were moist with sweat. He got out of bed and made his way to his desk, where a half-full mug of beer from the evening before sat. After draining off this tepid and bitter liquid, he slipped into his trousers, put on his boots, put a flashlight in his pocket, and went outside. He needed to breathe—to assess his vision, which had left on him a strong impression.

"Yes, a heart . . ." he murmured to himself, kneading his hands together.

The night was warm, silent. The building stood before him, vibrant, colossal—not far from complete.

Without turning on his flashlight, he walked along the north side, and then entered on the west, stepping carefully, like a man entering a temple—admiring the work he had done almost as if it had been done by another.

He went along one side quietly, eventually reaching that place where the altar would be and sat down, turned his head up, towards the unfinished dome. Through the great opening the night sky could be seen. Though there were a few wisps of clouds, stars shone.

Thoughts blossomed and faded in his perverse cranium, which was as fecund as a pile of manure and then presently, sitting there, he noticed a sound, like a dog moving about.

"Some animal must have got in here," he reasoned.

Just then he saw a shape pass quite close to him. A distinctly human shape, moving swiftly towards the Temple of Isis. He rose to his feet and, on tip toe, pursued, his huge ridiculous shadow cast behind him by the moonbeams which streamed in through the opening of the unfinished dome and which also allowed the figure to be seen, now hunched over against one wall.

The architect extracted his flashlight from his pocket, and flipped on the switch. A beam of strong light shot out, capturing the entity in its glare—a masculine figure with blond hair and a ragged moustache which wilted around his mouth reaching for an unshaven and cleft chin.

It was Fabrizio Fabrizi. At his feet lay a 25 kg sack of ammonium nitrate fuel oil, pink in colour, which he had just set down.

"Ah, it's you!"

"Yes, it's me," the other said, with a look that seemed to be traversing the border of anger and fear, hatred and madness.

"This building site is off limits to you. You are not welcome here."

Fabrizi gave off a short, ugly laugh.

"I've placed explosive charges at all the nerve centres of the building. When they go off . . ."

"You really are a mangy animal!"

Fabrizi stepped towards him menacingly.

"Help!" the architect shouted. "Help me!"

But as the sounds came from his mouth, the ex-foreman was on him, throwing him to the ground, muffling his mouth with his hand while digging his knee into his prosperous stomach.

"I'm going to kill you, wring the life out of you."

And Fabrizi set one hand around the throat of the other, began to squeeze him and would undoubtedly have actually killed him if it was not for the fact that the voice of Nachtman had actually been heard, for footsteps were already clattering over the marble flooring, proceeding towards them with excited speed.

"Worm," Fabrizi said, digging his thumbs into the throat of the older man.

Just then two of the Company of Good Men appeared—Sergei the Russian and Pedro from Columbia.

"Master," Sergei said in a dull voice. He took in the situation at a glance and moved towards them.

Fabrizi, seeing he was in danger, let go of his grip on Nachtman, who now gasped for breath, clutched at his throat.

"Get him," he croaked. "Get him."

But it was Fabrizi who attacked first, throwing a punch at Sergei, which landed squarely on the Russian's cheek. The brute only grinned. The tendons on his neck were like ropes. A moment later and the ex-foreman was in his hands.

Fabrizi tried to struggle, but it was useless. He was strong, but the other was vastly stronger and with ease twisted the Italian down to the ground.

"What should we do with him?" Pedro asked.

The architect recalled his dream and the words of Dr. Körn.

"Take out the bastard's heart if he has one."

And as it was said, so it was done, this thing being preserved in a casket and the architect set his energies to the great statue into which it was to be installed, which, with the help of a few assistants, he hastily made out of plaster of Paris, before having it cast into a single enormous piece of bronze—a thing which looked somewhat futuristic—sharp lines and deep grooves. The face was solemn, eagle-like—slightly imitative of Rodin's Balzac. The object was certainly grotesque and had a vague quality difficult to decipher, like some archaic representation of fertility or pain to be offered oil and blood sacrifice.

XXXIX.

As the structure neared completion, the number of workers rapidly decreased—all eager to sacrifice their physical beings to that demon-building whose entire purpose it would seem was to help depopulate the world. A solemnity ruled the place. Not only were there no smiles or laughter, but there was hardly any speech. Most communication was done by signs. A nod of the head; a jerk of an arm. The wind swept over the mountain, its lonely whistle audible as it blew over the crags and against the walls, interwrapped the towers.

One by one those workers disappeared, were transmuted, not into gods or trees, not into flowers or birds, but rather bricks dull-red in colour which mute, without even the echo of a whisper, found their place atop that grotesque megastructure, that drunken lump of stone and flesh.

The Company of Good Men, having been prohibited from sacrificing themselves, with promises of a special place amongst the elect, worked with an almost superhuman force and in the end, aside from the board members themselves, it was only these that were left, these formidable troglodytes who had, through continuous labour, through vast artificial means, become things it would have been difficult to call human. They seemed to make the earth quake when they walked and their craniums rested on huge necks which in turn descended into pillars of muscle. These fellows now gave up almost all sleep, only napping for ten minutes every now and again, and spent all their time up on the heights of the structure, putting in place the bricks that were hoisted up to them with a crane which was operated by Nachtman himself.

Enheim and Borromeo lent all their time, helped put into place those last blocks made from workers who but a short time before had been by their sides, and it was something marvellous indeed to see these individuals mounted atop the great building, crawling over its dome in excitement, fearless—recklessly going about the work as if the fate of the world rested in their hands.

The sun watched throughout the day; the moon at night.

And finally, the work was all but finished . . .

"We will place the last stone, the capstone, tomorrow," Nachtman said.

"And then it will be done," added Dr. Enheim, an odd, hollow note in his voice.

"Yes, it will be."

"And the real work can be begun. Gathering new recruits to our ranks and inaugurating a new era—when the people of the world can be united under our banner, be taught to adhere to our philosophy."

The architect ratified the statement with an affirmative grunt.

XL.

The mountain was tranquil.

Peter, having parked his car below, hiked up the trail, the small road that had been carved in the side of the natural elevation. He had been informed that the Meeting Place was to be completed that day, the capstone put in place, and he could not resist venturing to the site.

It was spring and flowers pushed themselves up out of the earth. A bird sang timidly in a tree and down below, in the valley, one could faintly hear the sound of the church bells of the distant villages strike the noon hour.

And yet this calm seemed somehow false—seemed to be tinged with a grim whisper and the sleepy trees and lazy grass seemed unreal, especially for one whose mind was constantly on man-made things, who had been brooding for long over that acropolis on the mountain from where he had once been banished.

He made his way up, and as he ascended, noted that all the trees at the higher elevation had been done away with, the earth ravaged, ripped away at—strewn with dislodged boulders and mutilated stumps.

As he rounded a bend, he looked up, was confronted by the site of an edifice such as the world had never known—a thing extracted from the wildest dreams, a nightmare harnessed and dragged into the physical world. He adjusted the glasses on his nose and for a moment stood there gazing at that gigantic place in the distance, violently coloured, as if it had been decked in the vestments of some scarlet woman, painted with blood, strewn over with the guts of its victims. It stretched out of the mountain top like some monstrous claw looking to snatch God from the very heavens. Strange spires sprang and lurched off from the sides, some of them looking like horns, others like tentacles. Its massive doors, which stood open, were like the gaping mouth of some obscene beast which could have swallowed entire four or six elephants at a time. The whole was capped by a dome, negligently clothed in strands of cloud, out of which jutted several snouts at the ends of which were rounded windows, like the eyes of a chameleon.

Peter could vaguely make out a small group of figures standing before it, and hurried his pace, putting one thin leg before the other, panting as he gained altitude, as he made his way up the steep and lengthy incline.

The trail was strewn with bizarre objects, the origin of which was difficult to determine: a plastic comb, the leaves of an old Bible, a large bone, the body of a dead cat;—and then pieces of broken, junked machinery—huge springs and sidecutters, tractor canopies and crankshafts, trapezoidal screws and nuts.

The young man mounted the trail as quickly as he could, drawn forward, not so much by his own will, as a necessity to be close to that great structure, to touch it—as certain foolish individuals are compelled to show themselves before angered bulls, even at the risk of being gored.

Out of breath, sweat dripping from his high forehead, he finally arrived at the south side of the building. The various dramas it had gone through could be seen like the various strata of the earth's surface, and it seemed as if the entire history of the universe, the entire history of the human race was written there, from its transformation from tadpole to its illusion of godhood—from the time when eukaryotic cells first appeared, to some distant future when men will have evolved into brains with wings, whose only link to other living beings will be their ability to defecate and procreate.

Instead of going directly to the entrance, which was on the east side, he decided to go around the building the opposite way, so that he could take the whole of it in undisturbed—which was a simple matter indeed, as the place was all but abandoned—like some zone that had been ravaged by a plague, the only beings presently apparent being those invested in the structure itself.

High up, in the form of gargoyles, the faces of its victims peered out, looked over the earth they were no longer a part of with apparent horror, sickening grins, twisted lips and hands that scraped against the atmosphere, seeming to search for their hearts which had long ago been vended, sacrificed at a blood-soaked altar wrapped in the tails of demons and dragons; and the whole scene was striking, for down below, to the west, sparkled the blue of Lake Lugano, while to the east a dramatic strip of Lake Como could be seen; and to the south Valle di Muggio, beyond which, in the distance, was the city of Milan covered with a dark sheet of pollution.

The structure was not beautiful. But powerful it was, in the same way that certain compositions, such as those by Hieronymus Bosch, though far from pretty, fill one with awe—an incongruity of fire and flesh, of knives dancing with naked limbs and featherless birds making love to the ears of dilapidated whores.

Peter walked along, fascinated, horrified—for this was indeed the building of his dreams, of his nightmares—a thing of mad grandeur, of ogee arches and umbels of carved stone—a thing of tortured flesh in ashlar masonry which made him dizzy to look at, so high were its walls, so soaring its towers.

He rounded the corner and was soon there at the main entrance with the board members, who were just finishing up a complex ritual which consisted of the sacrifice of a pair of doves, Nesler clumsily strumming on an acoustic guitar, and Enheim speaking an incomprehensible litany, responses being provided by those present, in syllables that tried their best to be enthusiastic.

Despite the warm weather, the men all wore thick overcoats over flowing dalmatics, the hems of which were embroidered with scarlet silk, while Maria wore a thick coat lined with white wool, in which her body, all skin and bones, was lost. Her hair, cropped short, was oily and caked with bits of plaster. Her eyes were two dying embers glowing in sunken holes—suns which had lost all heat and were ready to consign themselves to oblivion. A violent streak of white appeared in Dr. Enheim's once pitch-black beard and his eyes had a distant look in them, as if he were gazing off into other worlds. Borromeo's face, not long ago so well preserved, was marked with fissures and his lips were unnaturally swollen. He was unshaven, his prominent chin covered with tiny white bristles. He wore a pair of sunglasses and smoked a cigarette nervously.

It was only Nachtman who seemed to have grown younger. His face glowed. His small eyes twinkled. He walked about, gazed at his creation, swinging his large arms energetically and moving with agility his thin legs which were mounted in thick-heeled boots, giving him the look of some Venetian Duke from times gone by.

He greeted Peter as the latter approached.

"Ah, you are here to acknowledge my victory," he said haughtily. "I feel sorry for you—that you were not more obedient. But today is a good day, and I will bare you no grudge. Come, let us enter, so you can see what architecture truly is!"

The young man surveyed his aunt, said hello, and she cast on him a rather cold, lost glance, but did not speak or respond—seemed indeed not to even recognise him as the little party passed through the giant doors, from the outer sunshine to the inner chill. For though it was May, the inside was cold as a February night and Peter now realised why everyone had been dressed so warmly.

He shivered and looked before him. At first glance he could not perceive the boundaries of the interior, which seemed as if it went on forever—a place one might traverse for weeks on end without coming to its limits. And, due to the natural irregularity of design, to Nachtman's mania for splicing together organic shapes, the whole seemed a confusion, a chaos of moons and a conflagration of water. Some walls dripped with odd-coloured paint and others were ornately decorated with jutting hexagons, dug-in octagons, and optical illusions which gave a false sense of limitless depth. The floor tiles were modelled after those in the Basilica di San Giovanni in Laterano, making it seem like endless steps receding into the distance.

The place was huge—a world of its own which, though just built, seemed already haunted—by wandering souls, hungry ghosts—dispossessed spirits who wept in the walls and gazed from the ceiling through shadowy lenses. This vast mortuary chest was strung with horrible vibes and Peter felt as if his skin were being caressed by the soft hands of the dead—which were more subtle than cobwebs and lingered about his heart and soul, gently touching their ethereal chords.

The party wandered through a forest of columns, each one as large as the trunk of a five-hundred-year-old sequoia, with bases immense, mammoth pedestals on which rested those great fluted shafts. Maria seemed to float along, almost weightless—a dandelion clock carried along by atmospheric currents. Nachtman, Borromeo and Nesler spoke, their voices echoing through the vast space. Dr. Enheim stroked his beard as he walked, his steps somewhat unsteady. His belly sagged and Peter could hear him breathing through his nose and took note of his glassy eyes and quivering hands and indeed felt some pity for this man who was like one fallen from the sky, a being who had tumbled from the lofty clouds of his ideas to the lonely maze of the earth.

Peter gazed about him in amazement. Though most of what he saw had already been apparent in the plans he himself had helped to draw up, seeing them made reality had a profound effect on him.

"Come this way," Nesler said, stealing up to his side. "With this structure, my life finally has meaning and my only regret is that I was not able to work more vigorously towards its glory!"

And he guided the young man towards the northern flank of the building, to a side temple decorated with complex symbols of numerology, to a place which seemed like some odd altar to the God of Accounting, with zero ruled by Pluto and three Jupiter, with six aligned with carnal man and seven the Enchanting Virgin.

"This is the temple that carries my name," the man said, "the Temple of Nesler. This is where, in the future, the holders of knowledge of our system will teach the art of numbers, lecturing on the great harmonic sum."

And then there were other temples, each one denominated according to a member of the board; and others again, more impressive still, such as the temple of the Hunter Spirit, the interior of which was lined with animal skins, draped with bones—the walls frescoed with sheep caravans, gazelles, aurochs stampeding over abstract patterns that seemed to represent the night sky, handsome lakes—primitive forests populated by birds;—and then the flooring, done in green rubber, was reminiscent of fresh grass. And the Temple of Isis, where the inverted triangle, the sign of femininity and water was worshipped—a place where the walls were bedecked with ankhs; a small altar with a cow carved out of lime; then false sheaves of wheat, cast in plastic polymers and painted to look quite real. And then there was the Temple of Amun, the walls of which were embossed with Coptic writing and strange hieroglyphic designs, a dizzying array of plundered, mutilated symbolism brought there to be ground between the palms of this new cult which claimed its inheritance of the entire universe, claimed to be the direct disciples of both Christ and Buddha, of Mohammed and Lao Tzu.

After inspecting these for some moments, Nesler and Peter made their way back towards the centre, walking through a maze of male geometric energies, and rejoined the group. And soon together all arrived at the womb chamber, before the altar, which rose before them dark and fantastic, a thing that made Peter catch his breath in horror-tinged awe, his eyes fastened on the immense bronze statue of Körn, a monstrosity like that of the statue of Emperor Constantine which once dominated Rome, which looked on from the heights of the altar—an altar decorated with jacinth and surrounded by huge sticks of opoponax incense from which corkscrews of smoke spiralled heavenward. The face, though grave, seemed to be smirking and sneering through the smoke, and seemed vaguely infernal, a creature that had risen up from the bellows of the earth and, decked in the entrails of its victims, stood still hungry for further sacrifice. Horns of all sorts of animals, buffalo and stag, rhinoceros and narwhal, jutted out from the sides of the altar itself and the whole was painted with a red that made it seem like a waterfall of blood—a huge wound out of which poured so many lives, from poor Indian farmers to rich New York stockbrokers, their life-force whipped together and used to propel forth this great motionless machine.

Ostrich eggs also hung from the ceiling, for these would keep out spiders for the next hundred years. Chandeliers of fibulas and tibias hung on extravagantly long chains of beaten copper, and in these candles burned. Blotches of red and green, of lilac and Parma violet, fell on the floor, cast by those great stained glass windows, on which pseudo-biblical scenes were depicted, as well as mythological sequences.

Enheim cast his eyes high up, to the dome, where his daughter, a single brick, rested, her plump little hands seeming to be beckoning to him, her little mouth seeming to be casting on him a sad smile.

Far above, through the opening in the dome, a patch of blue could be seen. A large shaft of white light spilled through the opening. This was where the capstone, the last piece of the structure, would be laid and a few tiny shapes, mere ants, the Company of Good Men, were there dangling their legs from that magnificent height, waiting to put the stone in place.

Maria clung desperately to Nachtman's arm. She offered her lover a trembling smile and he squeezed her hand.

The architect turned to Peter.

"You see what I can do," he said.

"Yes, but at what cost?" the young man replied in a slightly irritated voice. "There is no one left to use the space."

"Disciples will come," Borromeo said knowingly.

"Yes, from here the message will be broadcast over the entire universe!"

Maria, in a voice hardly audible, spoke: "We only need to set the last stone in place, and all will be done."

"Only Peter and I are capable of operating the crane. I would like to witness the completion from within, so if my young friend would condescend to help us."

"Yes, I'll do it," Peter replied.

He drew himself away from the others, traversed the lengthy interior, walked through the huge iron front doors, those doors which had been refined from blood, and encountered the clean light of day. He took a deep breath, had indeed never felt so glad to see the blue sky above him, to be clutched by the rays of the sun. He made his way to the crane, a huge machine which rivalled the Kockums Crane in height and had a lifting capacity of around 500 tons—and indeed this immensity was well needed for the task at hand, for the stone, on which it seemed an entire village could be built, into which were carved astrological signs, Saturn's sickle and Jupiter's thunderbolt—

numerous magical symbols making the thing look like some object that had been uncovered from an archaeological dig—had to be lifted far above the earth and set atop that dome, in a manner not dissimilar to the cap stone of the Tomb of Atreus at Mycenae.

Peter mounted the great machine, climbed into its cab. The hook was already attached to the great block of stone and the only thing necessary for the young man to do was to start the engine and manipulate the levers. The latticed boom stretched into the sky and soon swivelled on its slewing baring. The stone was gradually drawn up from the earth, taken high into the atmosphere. Then the load moved along the lengthy boom until it hung over the dome. And slowly, gently, Peter lowered it until those of the Company of Good Men who stood waiting guided it with their powerful hands, with their formidable arms pushed the stone this way and that, and, as it was lowered in place, adjusted it, worked it into position until it sat tightly where it belonged. Then the hook was detached. The men waved their hands, let out a series of grunts, a few cries impossible to understand, flexing their muscular necks and distending their huge jaws.

Peter climbed out of the cab. He stepped back, raised his head, put one hand over his eyes and looked up at the structure, could see the Company scrambling up top.

And then a strange thing happened. Those men, those steroid filled beasts, disappeared.

The following instants dripped by, centuries, millennia seemed to exist in those seconds—the entire history of architecture, from brutish desert dwellers constructing their mud huts, to those mountains of glass which make up modern cities;—obsolete Mesopotamian settlements, Indo-Aryan temples and expressionist train stations all came toppling down together. The dome seemed to be opening its mouth, eating itself—a rabid demon gorging on its own flesh. Wax melting in a flame. The building began to crumble, to fall away like the vestments of some prostituted woman.

Indeed it could not withstand the weight of that huge stone placed upon its head, for, by the time the structure had reached this final stage of completion, the columns had been pushed far enough out of true to be of questionable usefulness and stonework had shifted.

Peter watched with a strange lack of emotion as huge chunks of the structure, a hail of brick, plaster and broken glass, spilled over the side of the cliff. Spires descended, walls collapsed, pillars threw themselves to the ground. A large cloud of dust slowly rose into the sky, momentarily blocking out the sun before gradually disappearing, parting, floating away.

And then all was still. Silence. In the distance the sound of goat bells.

The young man was neither surprised nor stunned. Certain disasters leave one cold, without emotion, speechless as if the heart were expelled from the body.

The structure was almost completely gone. Only the south wall still stood, reaching towards the sky out of a mountain of rubble like the hand of a drowning man. The great towers had dived to the earth. Those iron doors were on their faces, chewing on the ground and columns, all in pieces, lay sprawled out beneath piles of rubble.

High up in the sky, a jet airplane passed overhead, scarring the heavens with a streak of white. A breeze came and blew up a little dust.

Then, from that massive pile of ruins, which seemed like that of an entire lost civilization, there was a slight movement, like a rat in a heap of garbage.

A few stones moved, and then a creature emerged, white with plaster and the dust of bones, he appeared like some bizarre phantom—a massive torso balanced on stork-like legs. Forward he moved. He held his head up high and walked with measured steps, like an intoxicated man endeavouring to appear sober.

He approached the young man. Removing a handkerchief from his pocket, Nachtman wiped his face.

Peter stared at him in amazement.

"Unless funds can be come up with to start afresh," the former said in a surprisingly firm voice, "I am afraid I am going to have to throw in the towel on this project. As it is, it seems highly questionable whether I will be paid in full for the work I have done."

The other was silent.

"Anyhow," the architect continued, "as long as I can get a piece of meat to eat and a bottle to drink, I suppose I shouldn't complain."

"But . . ."

"Oh, don't bother."

He looked at Peter, blinked, shrugged his shoulders and then stalked off, made his way to the train, dusting off his body as he went. He climbed into the operating carriage, manipulated the controls, and slowly the transport began to slide away, had soon disappeared into a tunnel on its way down the mountain.

Peter stood frozen. Numb. His eyes wandered over that massive pile of rubble—that tomb that had buried not only his aunt and countless others, but seemingly the entire social structure and all the young man's vain ambitions as well.

A few clouds floated lazily on the sky.

A gust of breeze brought with it the smell of flowers and goat droppings.

Peter pushed his hair back away from his eyes, adjusted his glasses, turned, and proceeded to walk down the mountainside, towards the green valley below.

CPSIA information can be obtained
at www.ICGtesting.com
Printed in the USA
LVHW090035141219
640127LV00020B/12/P

9 781908 125088